A BOUND BY RAVENS
NOVEL

BOUND BY RAVENS

JESIKAH SUNDIN

FOREST TALES
PUBLISHING
Dystopian Fantasy and Faerie Tales

Text and Cover Design/Illustration

Bound by Ravens Copyright © 2023 Jesikah Sundin

All rights reserved.

ISBN-13: 978-1-954694-18-7

ISBN-10: 1-954694-18-0

Printed in the United States of America

Forest Tales Publishing, LLC

PO Box 84

Monroe, WA 98272

foresttalespublishing@gmail.com

This book is a work of fiction. Names, characters, places, and incidents are the product of the author's imagination or are used fictitiously. Any resemblance to actual events, locales, or persons, living or dead, is coincidental.

Cover design by Franziska Stern @coverdungeonrabbit

Case art and animal sketches by Lauren Richelieu

Character art by Alexandra Curte and Chicklen.doodle

Interior design by Forest Tales Publishing, LLC

To Otters...

You're not monsters. Don't let Irish mythology tell you any differently, you adorable, whiskered darlings.

Now I believe . . .

. . . in the faerie tales.

Irish Pronunciations

Oisín
(ush-een)

Tír na nÓg
(tier-nah-nogue)

Dobhar–chú
(doe-vur-coo)

Fionnán Ó Dair
(fee-yown-ahn / oh / dare)

Anlainn
(anne-lynn)

Primry Green
Seren
Stellar
Wind
Casino
Crescent
Street
Market
Beggar's
Hole
Ferry
Dock
Ferry
River Belesama

Kingdom of Carran

FENNEL MARSH

MINERAL SPRING

FIDDLING DUCK

DEN MERROW

WITCH'S COTTAGE

Caledona Wood

RIVER BELESAMA

TO THE EASTERN CITIES

TRAIN TRACKS

Chapter One

TARYN HUNT

I almost yawned, this next target was so predictable. So boring.

Small, meaningless jobs *still* added up on ledgers, though, thank the wishless falling stars, or I'd be owned by Black Beak until my brittled bones turned to dust. Probably would be, anyway.

A scowl deepened between my brows.

The middled-aged lady I'd been tracking since Crescent Street bent over a vendor's jewelry cart in a ridiculous poof of bustled blue skirts. She could hide an entire village of children under all that silk and petticoats. It was the belt purse now facing the crowd and feebly hanging at her hip that had me on the verge of rolling my eyes, though. The mainlander tourists, who were drawn to Seren's glittering gambling halls, night clubs, and fashionable street markets, stupidly immersed themselves in the notion that everything on the City of Stars was a high-class luxury—including their safety.

If only they knew.

The vendor's eyes drifted to mine. He arched a single brow, then looked away. I resisted the urge to snort.

This entire floating island above Caledona Wood, on the corner of two neighboring kingdoms, existed because of steam mechanics and magic. An entire pleasure island built on wild fantasies, run by the carrion crime syndicate—though the tourists didn't realize the latter. If the mainlander was pickpocketed, they saw it as part of the gambling games of Seren and laughed it off. The tourists were clearly glamoured before stepping off the steam-powered ferry. Why else would the poor be seen as a theatrical backdrop? A mere faerie tale to make the affluence seem brighter, more vivid?

And on that dream crushing note, it was time to get this over with and return to my castle in the sky. A paper-thin mattress, threadbare blanket, and a stale loaf of bread awaited my triumphant return.

Prepare to laugh at the fun of being robbed, lady in blue.

My gaze ticked by shoppers and rested on a man around thirty, his blond hair combed back, a top hat positioned perfectly so. A pretty boy from money who wore a hideous pair of red leather boots boasting small heels. A corner of my mouth hooked up.

Perfect.

"Hey, mate!" I barked to the man as he walked by. Blue eyes snapped to mine in surprise right before he tripped on the corner of a wooden crate I had eased into his path a second before. He lost his balance and threw out his hands. I fell back against the lady in blue, my back to her side, as if the man had pushed me.

"Keep yer disgusting fingers to yerself" I cried out, adding alley dialect to my otherwise middle-class born speech.

My target jolted upright and my fingers curled around the purse in a well-practiced motion, my hand hidden in all her silks. She would notice if I just yanked and ran.

To keep up the charade, I yelled, "Och, do I look like a common pleasure girl to ye?"

The man's face reddened and he frantically looked around at all the wide-eyed curious stares. He was probably an upstanding gent, but business was business. As I had hoped, the man scurried into the crowd, the gossipy hens following his flustered trail in excited whispers. With attention still diverted, I whipped around to face the woman, taking her purse with me and quickly stuffing it up my sleeve.

"Sorry, ma'am," I said with a wobbly curtsy. "Stars bless yer kindness to this poor lass." The woman had done nothing, but flattery was currency to mainlanders. I pointed toward my escape. "Me bairns are waiting on me. Bless ye," I added again for dramatic flair.

Her eyes softened, despite the annoyed tilt of her lips. Then she chuckled. Because of course she did. I wanted to roll my eyes so hard. Instead, with a faint tip of my head to the vendor, I turned on my heel. Once thick into the crowd, angling my way through Crescent Street Market, I tucked the coin purse into the satchel strapped across my shoulders. I may have cost the man a sale, but he'd have another. The merchant class didn't suffer here. Their day always ended in a warm home and full belly.

The exact life I had known until I was fifteen.

My gaze wandered over to *The Kettle's Thyme*, my parents' apothecary shop. Well, parents no longer. *You were a mistake*, my father's slurring voice echoed in my head. *You're dead to us*, my mother's voice snapped next.

I didn't miss my home, but I've been hungry for seven years now.

I could steal a meat pie from the baker's cart. But that would break rule two in the Thieves' Guild: do not steal from vendors and shop owners, only tourists. A fair rule, I suppose. It's not like the merchants could steal back from us, only recover. Plus, they're the honeytraps for the flies we catch.

Cutting between two carts, I stuck my hands into my pockets and slowed my pace. The alley between one of Seren's many gambling halls and nightclubs came into view. Three lads from a rival guild leaned against a brick wall while casing the evening crowds. We worked the same streets, breathed the same stars cursed air—unfortunately. A pair of light green eyes tracked me, a mock-flirty tilt to his lips when our gazes touched. I lifted a rude gesture in reply, making him grin. I wasn't in the mood for Finn Brannon.

I was *never* in the mood for Finn Brannon.

Before his friends could start heckling me, I slipped from the promenading crowds and into the shadows of an adjoining alley. Not too far up the narrow street, I angled around a brawl between two lads my age and a small bloodthirsty crowd trading bets.

Rule number one of the Thieves' Guild: no physical altercations between brethren or rivals. To murder a thief or put one out of commission, even temporarily, was the same as stealing from the boss. No one wanted to be the reason the guild lost money.

No. One.

Beggar's Hole was another ten-minute walk deeper into the warehouse district, where the Black Beak were housed. Old brick buildings towered above in all directions. Broken windows, kicked-in doors, pools of rust-filled water, and scattered rubbish combined with the aromatic scent of unwashed bodies and diseased hope surrounded me.

Ah, home sweet home. Made the cockles of my heart flutter just thinking about it.

Before the casinos, clubs, fancy balls, and high-end markets, Seren was an island of factories for the mainland, owned by the fae. Now it was part of the island's bygone industrial aesthetic for the tourists. Strange people, mainlanders.

"Taryn," a male greeted.

Tommy, a fellow mortal, appeared from the shadows and sidled next to me. An unlit smoke dangled from his mouth. I wasn't sure if I had ever seen him actually smoke. Weird, but who was I to judge?

"Good haul?"

"A jackpot," I mumbled dryly.

Tommy tossed an old coat button up in the air and caught it while we walked. "By the pissy look, I'll gander a day of easy pickings, yeah?"

I stopped and turned toward him. "What do you want, Tommy?"

The corner of his mouth ticked up. He jerked strands of blond hair from his hazel eyes before settling his sharp gaze on my lips. "We could be a team, you and I."

I snorted and started walking again.

Rule number three: do not get intimately or romantically involved with fellow brethren. Nobody adhered to this rule, though. There were rooms in the empty warehouses that *everyone* knew were for breaking rule three. Not that I cared. Never again would I put myself in that vulnerable position. The last and only time I fancied romance, I had given my heart to a boy who set me up to take his fall. And here I was, a raven bound thief to pay off my jail bonds as well as the fees Corvus paid to drop my charges, now disowned by my parents for falling for that boy's trick.

"Keep rejecting me, Taryn Hunt," Tommy said with an impish smile, the cigarette balanced between his teeth, the button tossed into the air again. "I like the chase."

I waved a dismissive hand as I ducked into an unmarked warehouse.

The only time the guild looked the other away was if two thieves took wedding vows. And that, my friends, would be worse than a shot to the head and surviving. Both debts would be combined and the partners were required to work together for the same pay-off fees as if working solo. Obviously, the guilds were brimming with married couples. I mean, how could one resist such an opportunity, right?

Around the corner, the guild master's door was open and I sighed, relieved. There were no rules against thieves stealing from fellow thieves. I reached into the satchel and pulled out the coin purse, my biggest catch, and sauntered closer. At the opening, I poked my head in. Danlio Baskens slouched over his desk, writing in a ledger while listening to a raven give a report. The point of his multiple pierced ears stuck out from his choppy black hair and ink stained the tips of his ring-clad fingers.

"Where was he last sighted?" Danlio asked the raven.

"The village Den Merrow, guild master," the raven replied from his perch atop a branch screwed to the desk. "Two days ago."

"And the ring, F624?"

The raven, identified by his tag numbers, cawed, "Never made it to the witch's cottage."

"Tell Corvus we have a runner and to send men. Kill on sight."

"Aye, guild master."

The raven flapped his wings and alighted into the air. I leaned onto the doorsill for F624 to fly past. Danlio peered up from the desk and stilled. His steely gaze wandered to the coin purse clutched in my hand, then he gestured with his head to enter.

"Shut the door behind you." Danlio rested his quill on his desk and held out his hand. I did as he asked before placing the purse onto his waiting palm. "Anything else?"

"I'm supposed to steal *more* things?" I opened my mouth in mock-horror. Danlio lifted an impatient brow, clearly not impressed with my performance. I emptied my satchel onto the desk—coins, pocket watches, necklaces, jewels, and a knife made of pure silver.

One by one he logged the objects, storing each item in a crate at his feet once finished. The tip of his quill touched each number while he added in his head. "Twenty-five credits."

"That silver knife is worth fifty credits, minimum. The coin purse was what, seventy-five, one hundred?"

Danlio's gray eyes flicked to mine. "Twenty-five credits, Taryn. You know I like you but argue with me again and it will be fifteen."

I crossed my arms over my chest and looked toward the dusty window to rein in my simmering anger. A muscle jumped along my jaw. "Twenty-five credits and a bigger job."

The elf chuckled under his breath. "Ballsy today, aren't we?"

I leaned onto his desk and lowered to eye level. "I'll get that ring for you."

Danlio cocked his head, a delighted smirk fluttering across his lips. "Yeah, love?"

"Yeah." I straightened with a smirk of my own. *Game on, arsehole.* "You don't shut your door to price up a daily catch. So stop being a gobshite and tell me what you're offering for the job."

"Two thousand credits."

The blood pumped hard in my chest. That was two years' worth of debt. *Two years.*

I could finally open my own apothecary shop.

I could weep.

But to appear unruffled, I collapsed into the chair opposite of him, rested my boots on the edge of his desk, and casually tossed out, "Tell me everything."

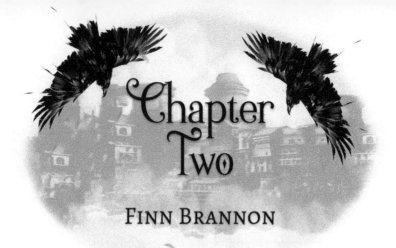

Chapter Two

FINN BRANNON

The day was dragging on and now rain threatened overhead.

Bloody brilliant.

I played with a small pebble I rolled between my fingers while sweeping a lazy gaze over the market. Tourists were thinning along Crescent Street and flocking to other money pits, leaving only locals who were busy with their weekly shopping. And why me and a couple lads from Corbie leaned against a casino wall to kill time before we were expected back at Primry Green. Or Prim, as we called it. A lovely park when Seren was in her manufactured sky island infancy, I was told. Now it was a junkyard filled with factory castoffs and the Corbies, Seren's eastside Thieves' Guild.

"That's her," Kalen, a fellow elf and my best mate, elbowed me in the ribs. "Lady Fianna Winslow."

I looked to where he pointed. A beautiful blonde-haired woman—in a flouncy red dress with a low-cut bodice cinched around a tiny waist—meandered down the market with the slinking grace of a cat on the prowl. "Not sure I fall for the 'he was taken against his will' tale. Feck, I'd willingly be her young buck."

Kalen snorted. Fianna meant "deer" in our fae tongue. Strange name for a mortal woman.

"Third lad taken from Corbie," Charlie said with a sad shake of his head.

We both arched a brow at the younger mortal for, once again, reminding us of this fact. What was it now, ten times since rolling off our mats and shoved into the cold to lift a handful of jewels and coins?

"Is that so, Charlie boy?" I asked dryly, "From Corbie, you say . . ." My eyes snagged on the large ruby necklace dangling from Lady Winslow's neck. "Well, isn't that a pretty thing."

"The poor lad who plucks that catch from her lonely breasts," Kalen playfully lamented. "Only pity I feel for his shite luck."

I tossed the pebble at Kalen who jumped out of the way. "Deep, sorrowful pity," I agreed. "Breaks my heart to know those three unfortunate lads, taken from their thieving ways in their prime, are now suffering beneath her—" A young woman walked by with a basket of produce, her eyes roaming down the full length of my body before settling on the curving slant of my lips. "Evening," I said with a dip of my head. Kalen lightly shoved me with a snort, knocking loose a lock of hair to fall over my eye. Ignoring my friend, I asked, "Need help carrying your load, love?"

She replied with a humored smile and continued on.

"Can I carry your carrots and potatoes straight to your bed, love?" Kalen said in a high, mocking tone once the girl was out of earshot. "Some days I hate your finely chiseled jaw and broad shoulders, Finn Brannon."

"You forgot my smoldering stare, Kal."

"Aye, you fine, devilish specimen."

Charlie huffed a laugh and rolled his eyes. "Stars, you two never stop, do you?"

"She's a looker," Kalen continued, not stopping, because no. "But you could do better."

Charlie groaned. "Not again."

"Last catch of the day." Kalen slung an arm around Charlie's shoulders and humorously pulled him in close. "Thieve a kiss within the next ten minutes, Finn, and I'll give you half of my dinner loaf."

I considered his bargain. "Five minutes and I get half your loaf tomorrow too."

"And if you lose," my mate threw back with a goading grin, "you'll sing a love ballad to guild master."

"That all?" I smirked. "He loves my singing."

"Makes him weep with joy, it does." Kal placed a hand to his heart. "Me too, mate. Me too."

Guild master hated my singing and my pretty face and I loved irritating him so. "Deal."

"Finn," Charlie warned. "You only have one year left."

"Relax your knickers, Charlie, or I'll kiss you instead."

With a wink, I sauntered into the market in search of the lucky lass. A mortal tourist, if I could swing one. Local girls were not as easily elf struck or swayed by guild boys. I rubbed the raven tattoo on my wrist, the mark that branded me the property of Rook, the Corbie guild boss.

One year left.

Lady Winslow caught the corner of my eye. She liked elven males and she liked them in their late teens and early twenties—her young bucks. As an added perk, I could take the burden of wearing such a heavy necklace off her near-bare shoulders . . .

Oh.

Stars bless me.

A girl in a pale pink gown, her ribbon-corded light blonde hair pinned up in curls and flowers, walked by and I spun on my heel to trail her movements. Lady Fianna Winslow had plenty of males to keep her lips warm. But this lass? She would remember me in her dreams this night.

Relaxing my body, I sauntered up to her side just as the sky opened up. Fat raindrops plopped on the cobblestone street. Well, shite. Before she ran for cover, I unclasped the bracelet from her wrist and let it fall to the ground.

"Lass?" I asked, hoping I sounded breathless and hurried as I crouched to pick up the pilfered piece. "This yours?" I straightened, unfurling my hand to reveal her bracelet. Her blue eyes widened, first peering at her silver and pearl chain, then flew to mine. Her mouth parted in the typical elf struck look of a mainlander mortal who couldn't blink away my predatory beauty—or wanted to.

The rain chose in that moment to dump and she squealed in surprise. Before she could dash to the covered walk, I grabbed her hand. "This way," I said simply and jogged to the nearest tree. One that so happened to be near Kalen and Charlie.

The foolish mortal didn't resist. Once beneath the tree's canopy, I fell against its trunk and tugged her closer, still holding onto her hand. "The bracelet, love?" I asked again.

"Yes, that is indeed mine." She chanced another look at me. "The bracelet belonged to my grandmother. A gift on her wedding day from my grandfather."

"Are you getting married?"

She gently shook her head and lowered her eyes demurely.

Turning her hand over, I caressed the pad of my thumb across her wrist. Then, I peered at her through strands of my fallen hair with a soft smile. "Allow me." I slid the dainty chain over her hand and reclasped the hook. "A pretty bauble for a pretty girl," I murmured.

A blush warmed her cheeks and she drew in a fluttering breath. She was perhaps twenty or so and clearly came from mainlander money. Girls like her always fall for boys like me. It was almost too easy. But that was the point. Tonight I would have a fuller belly.

The rain curtained around where we huddled beneath the tree. I remained still, waiting for her sentiments of gratitude. Mortals insisted on thanking everyone, a foolish tradition. Who wanted to be indebted to another? Humans, apparently. Especially nice girls who were taught to be overly pleasing, even to alley ruffians like me.

"How can I repay you for your kindness, sir?"

And there it was.

The corners of my mouth lifted in a flirtatious smile. Then I tapped my cheek. "A kiss."

"A kiss?"

I blinked softly. "A poor lad could only be so lucky."

She nervously laughed under her breath while looking around the quickly emptying market. Did she travel alone? By the way her gaze seemed to hunt for a familiar face, I was guessing no. But this was Seren and I was one of many indulgent fantasies this girl could entertain without loss to her reputation.

And, aye, I took advantage of that little detail often. I was a thief, not a gent.

"Well, I best be off," I said, to push her into a decision.

"Wait."

As expected, she placed her hands on my chest and bashfully rose on her tiptoes. Right before she reached my cheek, I turned my head to *steal* a kiss on the lips. Most likely her first kiss. Our mouths brushed and she sucked in a quiet gasp. I gave her a second to pull away. When she didn't, I cupped her face and pressed into the kiss. The girl practically went limp in my arms. They usually did. The fine, devilish specimen that I was.

But this was just about as exciting as watching Taryn Hunt feign being groped by a dandy—her usual trick of the trade. The accent was a nice touch, though.

These young, unwed mainlander girls were almost always the same. Well bred, sweet, innocent, thought a chaste kiss beneath a tree in the rain with a stranger was the height of forbidden adventure and naughtiness on Seren.

"Finn Brannon," a voice cawed above me in a branch.

Thank the stars.

The girl jumped back and pressed a startled hand to her chest. Her eyes shot to the raven. Then, to my amusement, she touched her flushing cheeks while her gaze darted frantically around the market and over the crowds pouring into the casinos and clubs. Without a magically bonded raven tattoo on her wrist from the Thieves' Guild, she wouldn't be able to hear the bird speak our tongue.

The bird flapped her wings. "Guild master summons you, Finn Brannon."

I turned my head to Kalen and Charlie and waved, to act natural when I replied to the raven. "I'll be right there," I hollered. The raven angled her head to watch me with one beady, black eye. What else did the damn bird want? "One minute!" I called out once more. At that, the raven swooped into the air and flew away. Knowing bird brains, she would probably tell guild master that I would arrive in exactly one minute. *Lovely.*

Returning my attention to the girl, I flashed her a corset-melting smile. "See you around, love."

I pushed off the tree and ambled toward my mates without a backward glance.

"Sir," she called after me. "What is your name?"

I peered over my shoulder and winked. "Finn."

"Finn . . ." she bit back the moony-eyed delight at forming my name with her just-kissed lips.

Aye, lass, say it as much as you like. Preferably when lost to pleasures.

Leaving her beneath the tree, I jogged over to Kalen and

Charlie.

"You're such an arsehole," Charlie said with a laugh.

"Finn . . ." Kalen sighed while batting his lashes.

I lifted my shoulder in a shrug. "A raven summoned me." I flashed them a smirk. "But I didn't mind the getaway excuse."

"That bad?" Charlie asked with a slight grimace.

I shrugged again. "Good girls kiss like good girls, Charlie boy."

"Why I only chase Corbie skirts." Kalen ruffled Charlie's rain-dampened hair. "And the occasional Black Beak. Rule three can kiss my arse."

Charlie glanced my way as we entered the alley. "Are you in trouble?"

"The feck if I know," I mumbled.

We tucked our heads down to avoid the rain as much as possible while traversing the maze of alleys in silence. A few minutes later, the junkyard arch appeared, announced by a rusted, half-hinged sign with the words "Primry Green" painted in scrolling letters. Inside, we hung a right and strode straight for headquarters in the nearest abandoned factory.

I paused at the door and turned toward Kalen. "I may have lost tomorrow's half, but you still owe me half of your loaf tonight."

"Aye," he agreed simply. "Fair is fair." Grabbing Charlie by the shirt, he hauled the lad off toward the bunks.

Better to get this over with. I pushed inside and moved across the brick floor in long strides. Guild master's office wasn't too far from the entry, either. At his door, I squared my shoulders and knocked.

"Ye're late," Niall, the guild master, hollered from the other side.

I turned the knob and stepped into the dusky, cluttered office and shut the door behind me. "The raven misunderstood me—"

"Ye think I care, Corbie?" he barked back. I knew it was a rhetorical question so I kept my smart reply to myself. "Sit, ye ungrateful bastard." I plopped into the indicated chair with a humored arch of my brow. "Rook has a job for ye on the mainland."

My back straightened. The mainland just below Seren meant primeval faerie forests and backward villages and cold nights beside monsters and spying ravens. I looked forward to these jobs, despite how Caledona Wood reminded me of how I was stripped of my home and no longer had family. And oh how I ached to set down roots and care for kin. The two things I wanted most in this world outside of my freedom. Two things my kind needed too.

One year left . . .

I wagered this job involved a witch's cottage. They were the main collectors and keepers of magical artifacts. Probably why I was summoned too.

I didn't like dealing with fae witches.

But refusal? . . . well, that meant more credits added to my debt and, that, alas, would not do.

"What does Rook need fetching?"

"A ring," Niall said with a gruesome grin. "Before Taryn Hunt fetches it first."

Chapter Three

TARYN HUNT

Three days of travel. Three miserable, cold days of travel with a spy raven on my trail and I had no idea how I was going to steal an ancient ring from an old crone. Or even what the ring looked like. The only description Danlio provided was "possibly a purple gem," as if that would open the starlit heavens and shine the radiant sun upon the chosen Black Beak target.

Apparently, the ring had the ability to control the weather. On Seren, sunny days meant market crowds and cold nights meant casino and club profits. Rain drowned out market sales. Travelers would often forgo the fun of gambling, too, not wanting to dirty up gowns and formal suits, favoring instead a private, indoor fire and a book.

Now wouldn't that be grand?

Certainly not my current state of luxury.

Mainlanders, try not to be jealous, but since the wee hours of the morning, I have hid in the underbrush and closely watched an old crone's cottage. Terribly fun. Best time of my life, if I may boast.

Stars . . . Help. Me.

I blinked and returned my devoted attention back onto the object of my present despair.

The small one-room cob and timber structure was crowned with thatch that was more a nest than a roof. Wisps of smoke curled into the air above the chimney and I sighed. What I would give to sit before that fire right now—

A shadow slipped between the trees beside the cottage and I perked up. Finally, a bit of intrigue. I craned my neck to better see her visitor when a familiar head of dark forest green hair popped into view.

"Stars, why him?" I gritted out. Ugh, he was the actual worst.

Per usual, the elf's hair was shaved close on the sides and back, the longer strands tied into a loose knot atop his irritating head. A chunk of angled hair, appearing almost black in the low light, fell lazily over one of his pale green eyes. His pointed ears were decorated in several piercings. And, because the male believed he was a strutting cock above the rest, his faded blue tunic sleeves were rolled up to his bicep while the front remained unlaced to expose a stretch of fair skin.

I rolled my eyes at the obnoxious level of his self-love. *Not all girls swoon over you, Finn Brannon.*

The Corbie wouldn't steal my catch.

Looking around for options to sabotage that annoying elf, my gaze settled on a couple of small rocks. The side of my mouth lifted. Finn was too engrossed in staking out if the crone was holed up in her cottage, that he didn't hear or see me slowly stand.

See if the crone finds you dashing, thieving arsehole.

I chucked a rock. The stone flew through the air and hit his shoulder. *Shite.* I was aiming for the window. Finn spun on his heel and I ducked, unable to hold back a snort of delight. A few seconds later, he returned to his mission and stepped closer to the cottage. Once more, I rose to my feet, lifted my arm, and threw another rock. It hit his calf and he dropped in surprise.

Well, bless me. A lass could get used to taking out arrogant Corbie males who tried to steal my jobs.

Finn stood and spotted me immediately, his teeth bared right before he emphatically mouthed, "Rule one."

I shrugged, lifted my arm, and hurled the last rock in my hand. Finn ducked and the rock, *finally*, hit the latticed window and sailed through. He jumped up, gaped at the window, his mouth moving in a stream of curses before he took off for the woods.

Sliding to a stop beside me, he crouched and angry-whispered, "Are you daft?"

"Appears Corbie sent a willing sacrifice to Caledona Wood to please the gods." I turned innocent eyes his way. "It's my stars blessed duty to help their cause. Nothing personal, yeah?"

He laughed under his breath, a humorless sound. "Careful, Taryn Hunt. We are not on Seren."

"Finally aware of your surroundings, are you?" I patted his arm. "Aye, Corbie made a good choice in sacrificing you to the faerie wood."

Finn's smile was both sensual and biting. "I can think of several pleasant ways to punish your smart mouth, love." He leaned in and I leaned back with a snarl of warning. "But first," he whispered roughly, his otherworldly eyes dropping to my lips a beat before flashing to mine. My pulse fluttered in an act of betrayal. Stupid pulse. "I need to catch something far prettier than your mouth."

I didn't even have a chance to reply. The bastard had lightened on his feet and ran. Toward the cottage. He was racing toward the cottage—

And it hit me.

The crone never appeared outside.

Sweet suns above. I either killed her with the rock, struck the old witch down unawares, poor dear, or . . . she wasn't home. I scowled and clenched my jaw. This whole stars blasted time she wasn't home while I hid behind a bush like a moping lunatic.

Getting to my feet, I charged after Finn, determined to finish the job. That preening elf would *not* steal a closer-to-freedom future from me. I had an apothecary shop to open, hopefully one that would put my parents out of business. Seven moons, I missed tending a garden and creating tinctures, salves, teas, and poultices.

Finn softly pushed on the iron ring handle, then stilled in the doorway. His jaw dropped; his eyes went wide. I was ready to angle past him when the room came into full view.

"Holy mother of stars," I breathed.

Hundreds of taxidermized skunks lined the walls, the shelves, hung from the ceiling, piled around the compacted dirt floors. All wearing wigs that appeared to be made of genuine hu-

Witch's Skunk Ornament

man and elven hair in a wild myriad of fashions. They were out-
fitted in a wide range of clothing too, from ornate gowns and suits
to tattered peasant garb.

Were these . . . *trespassers?*

A shudder wended down my spine and flushed across my
skin.

"Two thousand credits," I whispered to myself. I could do
this. Maybe.

Finn's head whipped my way. "That's what Black Beak offered you?"

I nodded my head and he swore. "What's your offer?"

"Twelve hundred," he mumbled with a disgruntled roll of his
eyes.

Unable to hold back a smirk, I pushed past him and stepped
into the creepy cottage. A musty, rotting scent hit my nose and I
grimaced. Finn's light steps padded closely behind mine. I moved
in deeper, horrified by all the sights around me, and accidentally
kicked over a skunk.

I slapped a hand over my mouth.

"Sorry," I whispered. "So sorry." Bending down, I righted
the girl skunk and gagged at the feel of her curly blonde hair falling over my fingers. *Gods* . . .

Standing back up, I peered around the space to get my bear-
ings. A table took up one corner, a lit hearth nearby. The warmth
was a lover's caress on my chilled skin.

Wait . . . the hearth was lit. While she was away?

My body pivoted toward the bed and I backed up a startled
step and right into Finn, who caught me before I unbalanced us

both. His fingers wrapped around my arms and, for a traitorous moment, I was happy for the company and sense of protection— even his.

The old crone was curled up in a small bed, her chest rising and falling in sleep. The window breaking didn't wake her? Maybe she was deaf. Or was this a trap? Did I have a choice in caring? To fail this mission would be several steps backward in achieving my freedom.

I turned and locked eyes with Finn for a couple charged seconds. Those pale green eyes slid to the crone, his eyes widening for only a fraction of a fluttering heartbeat before narrowing, and a sly smile hitched up the side of his mouth. He dipped his head in a curt nod. Then we flew into action. Too much was on the line to back out now.

He crept to one end of the cottage and I to the other, careful not to make a sound. Naturally the brave lad went to the side away from the witch, closer to the door.

Heart in my throat, my fingers combed through object after object. Drawers, filled with disgusting, dried insects and moth wings, creaked open and close, and I winced each time. Atop cabinets and placed haphazardly on shelves, in-between skunks, were chipped porcelain dishes full of coins, leaves, petals, and odd end jewelry pieces. I rifled through the earrings, pendants, and rings, not sure of exactly what an enchanted "weather" ring looked like. So, I pocketed five possibilities, just in case. I peered over my shoulder and watched as Finn pocketed items here and there too.

My pulse was beating so fast, I swore it alone would wake

the crone with its endless thumping. Swallowing back the tightening knot in my throat, I slid my wary gaze to the bed and cocked my head. A glinting light twinkled in the thin stream of sunlight. My body deflated. A ring with a purple gem was securely resting on one of the witch's fingers. Well, shite. This was just lovely. I shot a look Finn's way, but he was studying contents in jars, his back to me.

"Two thousand credits," I whispered to myself. "Two thousand credits."

The taxidermized skunks seemed to scream their warnings as I quietly approached the bed. I could feel their bulging, glazed eyes following my every doomed step. At the bed I drew in a slow, fortifying breath, pushed back the nausea nipping at my gut, and reached out. This was the ring. The stars were *clearly* on my side, so of course it was the ring.

My teeth clenched until I thought they might crack.

It was now or never . . .

With the ghost-whispered touches of a professional thief, I maneuvered my fingers beneath hers and involuntarily shivered at the feel of her dry, papery skin. How old was this crone? Hundreds of years? Thousands? The tips of my fingers positioned around the top of the ring and the bottom of the band and tightened. Grip secure, I nudged it a hairbreadth toward freedom. My eyes snapped to her face and stilled. Wrinkles deeper than tree bark grooved her skin. Her white hair frizzed in a wild halo around her pillow-tucked head. Still she slept.

Did she take a slumbering draft?

Was she perhaps a disguised princess waiting for her true

love's kiss?

I tugged on the ring with slightly more force. Thankfully the target object was larger than the crone's thin, bony finger. Ready to vomit, I slid the band over her knuckle, down her long, clawed fingernail, and . . . my lungs collapsed. Clammy beads of sweat had gathered on my forehead and my hands began to subtly tremble.

A relieved laugh was forming in my belly. I found Finn watching me closely, his gaze affixed onto the ring in my open palm. With a goading tip of my head, I turned from the bed toward the door and—dear forest gods, milky eyes locked onto mine.

I squeaked. The kind of squeal that released one's soul from their body to forever float away.

A yellow-toothed grin crept up the crone's cracked lips.

I jumped back, hitting a bookshelf, the startled force knocking the ring from my hand.

No, no, noooooo.

It rolled directly toward Finn who swaggered over, plucked it up from the floor, tipped his head at me, then dashed out of the door.

"You arsehole!" I screamed, forgetting all about the witch. That was *my* freedom he stole. The crone cackled and I jumped again.

Not wasting another breath, I ran from the cottage. The cackle only grew louder once my feet hit the path and the sun squinted in my eyes. My heart was galloping at breakneck speed, my legs pumping like pistons on a steam engine. By pure rage alone, I caught up to Finn and, with a roar, jumped onto his back and tackled him to the ground.

Our bodies hit the dirt with matching grunts. We rolled over ferns and grass, slowing with me straddling his waist. The ring popped up into the air. I leapt for it. Finn grabbed me by the shirt and yanked me back down. My back slammed into the spongy forest floor. The bastard then crawled across my heaving body to reach my catch. So, I did what any decent lass would do—bit his arm. Hard.

"Feck!" He hissed. "What the hell, Rynnie? Rule one!"

"Rynnie?" I screeched in a war cry. We were beyond rule one at this point. "Hand over the ring, *Finny*, or I'll do more than bite your arm."

"Oh, love," he crooned, bringing the smug tilt of his lips close to mine. "The way you seduce me."

"Seduce—"

Then he kissed me.

He.

Kissed.

Me.

Tongue and everything.

Laughing, he pushed off the ground while I lay in open-mouthed shock. The cackling sound of the crone grew louder. My fury was two seconds from combusting in an epic explosion. I rolled onto my stomach and shoved off into a run after that in-furiating male to rearrange his balls. But my muscles froze while in a half-step, one foot off the ground. Magic buzzed down my limbs and across my skin. Finn was in a similar shape, my only consolation. If I were to be turned into a creepy skunk ornament, he better stars damned well be too.

"Pets," the crone said in a deep, raspy voice. "You stole my sister's beloved heirloom."

I was going to be sick.

Chapter Four

FINN BRANNON

I was born to become a skunk ornament in a crone's cottage, apparently.

This was the true purpose of my existence, the fate-weaving arseholes.

At least Taryn Hunt would join me in a taxidermized afterlife. A small comfort, but my competitive spirit would accept no less in this doomed situation.

The fae witch practically floated over the ground to where I stood paralyzed. Her decaying grin widened. Foul air from her wheezing breaths stung my nose. "She will give you a choice, pretty elf."

My heart dropped into my stomach.

She?

What in the stars was this creature? She was no ordinary crone, of that I was certain.

The witch dragged a nail down my cheek and I held her

all-seeing milky stare. "Do her bidding, faeling, and your curse will be light. Or . . ." She dragged that same nail down my exposed chest and licked her lips. "Refuse the task and be cursed to the Otherworld and back, twice for you and thrice for not protecting your mortal mate."

Was she part of a Sisters Three? Aye, she had to be. Clearing my tightening throat, I called on my memories of living in the faerie wild and living among the Caravan fae before I was dumped on Seren as a wee lad of thirteen. A Sisters Three were no mere fae or lowly forest witch but a triple goddess who shifted into the various stages of a female's life: maidenhood, motherhood, and the crone years.

I opened my mouth and promptly shut it. Her words caught up to me.

My *mortal mate*? A laugh wanted to bubble up from my sickening gut, but I had a curse to dance around first. Time for laughing into my grave afterward.

"Fair Mother," I said in the stronger lilting voice of the fae—

"It is the Maiden who pleads on your behalf, lad. Make no mistake." Her cackle rose the hair on my arms. "It is *her* ring you stole." A ring she scraped from my palm and placed back onto her bony finger.

"Then fair Maiden who speaks through the Crone," I continued in a thicker brogue, grateful Taryn, my future skunk mate, remained quiet, "what is your bargain?"

"Finnan Ó Brannon of Primry Green and Taryn Hunt of Beggar's Hole," she wheezed in delight and turned Taryn's way. "One foot of freedom for each transgression is your curse."

With a snap of her fingers, five rings Taryn had lifted flew from her pockets and into the air. Three rings, two necklaces, a pair of earrings, and two hair combs departed my clothing at the same time. The stolen items gently fell into the crone's hands and my throat bobbed.

"Fifteen belongings you have taken. Fifteen articles of magic not yours." The witch wheezed a laugh. "And so you will only know fifteen feet of separation from the other."

The air tightened in my burning chest.

Taryn groaned, a sound like she was in her final death throes and fighting for one last breath to beat me to death first. That girl was an angry gust of wind. And probably *would* take my soul with her into the Otherworld if given half the chance.

"Crone—"

"And the bidding?" I asked, interrupting Taryn. *Hush, mortal. Let the fae have an adult conversation.* This was the Maiden's lighter curse, which meant, there was a way to break it. My pulse trilled at the possibility.

"Three tasks you are offered, my pets. Three tasks, no more, no less. Three magical objects you must bring me, three magical objects not touched by your magic." She lifted one finger. "The tooth of a Dobhar-chú." A second finger joined the other. "The ruby Amulet of Oisín." A third finger glared back me. "The Eye of Lugh in the tower of Corvus Rook."

My heart dropped into my stomach. *Corvus Rook?*

Was she suggesting that Corvus and Rook were one and the same? Or worked together?

"Your curse shall break," the Crone continued, "only when

all three objects are returned to me."

The last word barely dropped from her rotting tongue when an Otherworld's misty fog swirled around her and the cottage until only forest remained. I collapsed into a giant fern the next second. Taryn fell not too far behind me.

But my body didn't lay still for long.

It whipped through the air in a snapping tug in Taryn's direction.

I had two panicking heartbeats to figure out what was happening right before our stood-more-than-fifteen-feet-apart crash.

Her elbow hit my ribs and my head hit her shoulder. A beat later, we landed on the ground beside the other. A moan left my chest. I gasped for breath. Next to me, Taryn rolled into a sitting position and rubbed her shoulder.

"This can't be real," Taryn mumbled to herself. "Not again."

I tilted my head her way, brow arched. "A regular with attachment curses, are you, lass?"

"What?" Those dark brown eyes of hers narrowed on me. They were a lovely shade, like the dirt of a freshly dug grave—mine, apparently. She loosed a long, pained breath. "What in the blasted stars are you blathering on about? No. Never mind." She lifted her hands to stop me from replying. In a huff, she shoved to her feet and started to march off.

I lunged for her leg. No thought, just pure adrenaline. My fingers curled around her lower calf, abruptly halting her momentum. She fell with a solid thwump, then growled. A loud, guttural sound.

Her face, now covered in dirt, whipped my way. "Rule one!"

I crawled over to where Taryn ate the forest floor, rolled her over, then pinned her hands above her head and her legs down with mine before she could charge off again. Lowering my face to hers, I gritted out, "Did you hit your head too hard, love?"

"Get off me!"

"So you can stomp away and anger the magic binding us together?" I laughed darkly under my breath. She bucked her hips, screaming through clenched teeth. But I held steady. "There is no avoiding this, Rynnie," I warned.

"Go pound stardust, Finny."

"We are owned by different guilds and failed a large job. One of us *will* be hunted down."

The body beneath mine went limp at those words.

Our heated eyes locked.

The waist length, dark brown braid, usually draped down a shoulder, coiled on the ground beside her face. Flyaway strands framed her fevered cheeks. Her chest heaved against mine, the air between us charging with storm-building energy, and I almost forgot what I was thinking. Stars, the softness of her body moved beneath mine. And that anger-flushed mouth currently pressed into a firm line . . . I had kissed that mouth to shock her, part of my getaway plan. But I could still taste the sweetness of wild strawberries on her tongue.

"Finn . . ." her harsh, whispered breath fluttered across my lips and the blood in my veins rushed at the rough sound.

I lifted a corner of my mouth. "Begging for another kiss, love?"

"You can kiss my arse, *love*."

I grinned. "There are worse ways to spend fifteen feet of

freedom."

"Get. Off. Me," she seethed.

"Will you be a good little unicorn beam of sunshine and not run?"

"Unicorn—" She groaned. "I'll sit fourteen feet from you."

"Ten, in case you fall backward."

"Are you kidding me?"

"No," I said, quite serious, though I was not.

"Why would I fall backward?"

I lifted a bored brow. "Pixies bent on mischief. A feral badger. Murderous acorns falling from assassin oak trees."

She rolled her eyes. "I'll take the risk."

"Twelve feet, then. Not a centimeter more."

"Thirteen."

"Eleven." My gaze lazily drifted down to her lips. "Or I hold you down like this for our entire conversation. I'm not suffering."

"Fine." My eyes snapped back to hers. "Eleven feet. Now get off!"

I lowered my mouth closer to hers, delighted by the quick intake of her breath, and whispered, "Good girl."

Releasing her hands, I pushed off the ground and scooted away a couple of feet before she could attack. Taryn distanced herself another several feet and wrapped her arms around the knees she pulled to her chest. We couldn't accurately measure without a yard stick, but that wasn't the actual point of our bargaining.

Those lovely dark brown eyes pinned me from the shadows of a large tree. I could get lost in those doe eyes, if she weren't my rival permanently attached at my hip, for better or for worse . . .

My thought trailed off as a new one hit me square in the gut.

Holy stars.

That would work. It would buy us much-needed time. Convincing my future bride, though? No chance in a black hole's light. Still, the power of love-to-stay-alive compelled me.

"Taryn, my sweet whiskered alley rat, the one my soul calls Rynnie, I can't deny our hot, sparking chemistry a second longer." Her face fell in a here-we-go look that threatened a laugh to break through my clearly irresistible charm. "You keep seducing me, lass, despite my protests—" A muscle jumped along her jaw "—and, so, to save my tarnished reputation, I have decided to accept your proposal." Placing a hand to my heart, I theatrically whispered, "Aye, I'll marry you."

Chapter Five

TARYN HUNT

For a few seconds, I couldn't process the hundred different thoughts racing through my mind. Then I started laughing. Deep, rolling laughter at the absurdity of his backward proposal. I was on the verge of splintering apart. Angry tears burned behind my eyes.

I had lost the ring.

I had failed this job.

Corvus could send men after me, to shoot on sight, like the first Black Beak who was offered this job and ran.

And because the stars were obviously in love with me, I was now cursed to co-exist beside this ridiculous excuse for a thief, let alone elf, until we found those even more ridiculous items for the senile crone with multiple personalities—who also happened to have conveniently disappeared. Where would we find her cottage should we retrieve her requested objects? What if the objects weren't real?

Finn leaned back on his elbows, legs stretched out before him. A pretend fae god lounging in the faerie wood, believing that his unnatural beauty would bring the world to his feet. I had to admit, albeit grudgingly, that he was fine looking, far more than most elven males I knew. As if reading my thoughts, those arrogant lips slanted in a flirty smile.

"By the come hither look in your eyes—"

I scoffed. "Murder eyes, Finn."

The smile widened. "I'm flattered you'd kill for me."

Stars blasted riddling fae. Always a game of wit with them.

But this wasn't a game.

The tears I was holding back rimmed my eyes. Another boy who set me up to take his fall. Our separation in the cottage was too easy. He must have seen the ring on the crone's finger and waited for me to do the dirty work.

The smirk faded from his face as he watched the emotions fly across mine. "Marriage will protect us until we can break this curse."

"No."

He sighed. "Taryn, listen to reason. Our vows can include our divorce bargain too."

"You saw the ring," I gritted out. "You let me take all the risks, stole my catch, and then left me to face her alone."

His chest rose and fell, a sliver of guilt darkened his pale green eyes. "If we are married, we will be forced to work together."

"I know how marriage works in the guilds, Finn Brannon!" My fingers clawed into the dirt, wishing I were clawing out his eyes instead. "You want to know why I said, 'not again?'" I paused to make sure I had his rapt attention. "Because the last boy who kissed me had used me to do his dirty work and abandoned me when caught. He wanted to marry me, he said. Wanted to be mine forever. But he needed the money first. Said my savings weren't enough for the vows. I was fifteen and didn't know the fae could marry without priests or witnesses." A traitorous tear slipped down my cheek. "I didn't want to steal. I just wanted to be in love and plan my wedding. But his coercion magic convinced me to bring my family's entire savings to him, not just mine, and steal from a casino. He got away with all the money and I was arrested then disowned by my family."

"His name," Finn said on a dark, thundering whisper.

"Oh because you're so much better than him?"

He bared his small canines at me. "A hundred times better than him. A thousand times."

"You saw the ring and you let me take the fall," I shot back. "All you fae are the same, preying on mortal girls for your amusement and gain."

"His name, lass."

"I will give you his name when you earn it from me."

His eyes lit up. Faeries and their bargains. *Gods . . .*

"Deal."

"That's it? No apology for your own self-centered—"

He snorted. "Oh please, love. Like you wouldn't have stolen the ring from me or abandoned me to the riddling whims of the Sisters Three too. I'm no gent. You're no lady."

Sister's Three?

"You set me up!"

"No, Black Beak did," he threw back. "I had nothing to do with you being here, the debt you owe, nor did I make you do anything against your will. Thieves' business, that's all."

I deflated because he was right. And I hated that he was right. "You still kissed me."

"Aye," he said with a humored tilt to his lips. "And I'd do it again, Taryn Hunt."

We studied each other in the dappled light, a slow perusal, a calculating glint, a curiosity. The lullaby hush of the forest wrapped around me and I suddenly became aware of every bobbing fern frond, each swaying branch, the chirp of birds and insects. How many faeries were listening to our conversation right now? And why did he have to look so beautiful among the greens and trees, as if he were formed from their magic? Maybe he was. He certainly knew how to bargain with a crone and his accent changed when doing so. Was he born in Caledona Wood?

A sigh, that was more like a breathy growl, left my tightened chest. I couldn't believe I was considering marriage to a thieving elf. But we would be hunted if we didn't return soon. Spy ravens were probably already relaying how we lost the ring.

"A Black Beak was assigned to steal the ring before me and ran the moment he hit the mainland." I licked my lips and blew out another heavy breath. "Guild master gave orders to send men and to kill on sight."

Finn swore. "How many days ago?"

"Three."

"So, mercenaries are already crawling these woods on a hunt for a raven bound thief."

It was a statement, not a question. "If we marry—"

"Thank the stars," he said and fell back onto the forest floor with a dramatic thwump.

"If we marry," I said again, "It is in name only and with a divorce bargain."

"Lass, do you know the fae mate bond laws?"

My heart jolted to a stop. "I will *not* become your soulmate and there is no bonding."

"Calm your lovelorn heaving breasts." He rolled to sit, crossing his legs beneath him. "I'm talking about a bonded bargain."

"I thought the fae only *bonded* with their fated mates."

He studied my eyes with a soft intensity that shivered down my spine. "The making of soulmates is a magic not of this world but of the one beyond. There is no choice in fate, aye?" I faintly nodded in reply. "Elves live thrice as long as mortals. Some even longer," he continued. "And still Folk rarely find their True Mate. And not all True Mates desire the other despite their tethered souls."

They could reject their fated mate? Oddly, I found that comforting. "Fine. What are the laws, then?"

"Like mortal wedding vows," he continued, "the fae laws care not a wit if we're in love or in lust or not at all. Binding is ruled by a primal magic. One that makes some Folk temporarily territorial, aggressively so, or mad with lust." My brows shot up. "Just a wee bit dangerous. And why, by fae laws, the newly bonded are given fifteen days to strengthen and settle their new relationship. No work can be demanded of them."

My mouth fell open.

"Since we fae get dramatic with term limits," he said with a crooked smile, "eternity being a favorite, naturally, those bonded under marriage agreements can dissolve all wedding bargains within the first five days as a safeguard. Any transfer of money or property doesn't officially happen until the sixth day. And," he added, "if marriage binds are broken, the magic prevents rebinding."

"How have I not heard of this?"

"You've been a Black Beak since you were fifteen? So, like four of five years now?"

"Seven, arsehole."

He smirked. "How many fae marriages do you know?"

"No one marries in the Thieves' Guild."

Finn slowly nodded his head. "Why do you think they pool the debts together and only pay off as if one?"

"Ancient moon magic," I drolled.

"Ancient moon magic," he confirmed.

"What? Really?"

He started laughing and I wished I had more rocks to throw at him.

"Be serious, *Finny.*"

"Ravens, one of the oldest fae, are sacred creatures to Faerie Folk," he began, more seriously. "They See the future and the past, guard our fates, and guide us into the Otherworld. The old fae also can't lie. Since the first breaths of time, we have made vows and bargains in their name for these reasons. Mate and indentured slave bargains, *Rynnie*," he said slowly, as if talking to a village idiot, "are bound by ravens. It's how the Thieves' Guild has ownership over us too."

The muscles of my stomach clenched. "I am fae bonded to the Thieves' Guild . . ."

"Aye, as master and slave, until we are debt free when Corvus or Rook are required by fae laws to release our binds according to their bargain."

"I didn't have a choice!"

He shook his head. "There's always a choice, lass. You chose the lighter bargain, even if you didn't fully understand all the details."

My mind was spinning. "The fifteen days I was given to acclimate to the warehouses and brethren after my charges were bought—"

"Fae laws. Corvus was given the same."

"Holy shite in the sky," I breathed. "They can't hunt us down then, can they?"

His wide grin was all the confirmation I needed. "Fifteen days to break our curse, then we go our separate ways."

I rolled my eyes. "Fifteen feet of freedom. Fifteen transgressions. Fifteen days per fae laws. You fae and your riddles."

A preternatural gleam brightened Finn's pale green eyes. "Imagine if we only stole the target ring?" I shuddered. "Aye, the Sisters Three knew we were in Caledona Wood the moment we arrived. It was no accident the Crone woke only when the fifteenth item was taken."

My pulse kicked into a gallop at what he was insinuating. We were *not* fated for this curse—or for anything. That was absurd. But, for a Seren alley boy, he knew an awful lot about the ways of the fae, other faerie creatures too. "You were once a wild fae, weren't you, Finn Brannon?"

He considered me with a sharp eye, then lifted one of his trademark smiles. "The way you seduce me, love. Of course I still want to marry you. Make an honest male of me, Rynnie."

I groaned. He was such a self-absorbed eejit. "Fine, I'll make an honest male of you."

The elf crawled on hands and knees to where I sat, as if groveling before me, a wicked slant to his lips. His eyes steeled onto mine through fallen strands of his dark forest green hair. And stars, the sensual way he moved flushed hot down my body despite the betrayal I felt. No, I couldn't let him charm his way into my good graces.

Finn settled on his knees before me and took both of my hands. Lifting one, he gently kissed the raven tattoo on my wrist.

"Name only," I reminded him, and I swore at myself for how breathless my voice became.

He just winked. "I, Finnan Ó Brannon, mate bind myself to you, Taryn Hunt, for as long as we remain under the fifteen feet of freedom curse. I enter these binds without coercion and vow to put you before all others until we go our separate ways."

My mouth went dry. The heart in my chest was thumping violently against my ribs.

Clearing my throat, I awkwardly croaked out, "I, Taryn Hunt, mate bind myself to you, Finnan Ó Brannon, for as long as we remain under the fifteen feet of freedom curse." His lips slightly parted, as if he were genuinely affected by my words. "I enter these binds without coercion," I said more softly, a caress of breath pulsing against his, "and vow to put you before all others until we go our separate ways."

Warm magic drizzled down my limbs and settled onto my wrist. Our fingers remained knotted together in a bargain struck. I was about to pull away when I watched, part in horror, part in fascination, when the mark of a raven appeared on my wrist. One that soared beside the tattoo branding me the property of the Thieves' Guild.

I yanked my fingers from Finn's and abruptly stood. "So where can we find the tooth of a Dobhar-chú?"

Finn blinked back a daze he was apparently in and met my waiting gaze. But he looked at me as if for the first time, the pale green of his eyes alight with an intensity that quivered in my veins.

"Fennel Marsh," he answered in a faraway voice. "A day's walk from here."

Gone was the flirty humor and playful banter. Finn appeared shaken—gutted. A chill scraped down my spine. Had I bargained myself into a trap? Or was he beginning to go temporarily mad from the bonding?

Swallowing back the sob still knotting in my throat, I asked, "What is a Dobhar-chú?"

"The Otter King, the low fae call him."

"We are in search of a monstrous otter?"

"Not an otter, but not *not* an otter."

"Right." Stars, I was going to bash my head on a rock if I had to endure one more fae riddle. Tugging on the hem of his shirt, I gestured toward the trail. "Let's go."

I needed to move or I would curl up into a fetal position and angry cry myself to sleep.

Freedom had never felt so out of reach, the idea a fool's hope. In just two sentences, my debt became Finn's debt and his debt became mine. Worse, for the next fortnight or longer, we couldn't escape each other.

A scream scorched ash in my gut and clawed up my throat for release.

I was now raven bound to two fae thieves and on the hunt for a bog marsh otter monster.

Chapter Six

FINN BRANNON

I loathed bog marshes.

Mud filled my boots and squished between my toes. I swatted away a cloud of gnats while spitting at the few who blew in with my breath. A loud plop sounded to my right, too loud to be an air bubble, and I halted, putting my hand up for Taryn to stop too. Gripping the spear I carved from a tree limb last night—one for me and one for Taryn—I swept a sharp gaze over the tall reeds and dead, moss-draped trees.

Dobhar-chú were sneaky monsters for being the size of a juvenile dragon. With rough fur the color of the bog's clay mud, they were difficult to see. Usually one had to rely on their scent: fresh baked cookies beside a pile of rotting rubbish. Most were lured in by the sweetness while believing the foul stench was merely the marsh itself. The overwhelming licorice fragrance of the wild fennels here, however, masked almost every scent around us.

Spotting the red glint in the Otter King's eyes was the only advantage we presently had.

But he also wasn't the only dangerous creature to roam the bog.

With a flick of my hand, I gestured for Taryn to continue forward. I drove the butt of my spear into the mud as leverage to drag my boots another step.

My mind, since binding myself to Taryn, had been as thick as mud too. In the middle of her saying her vows back to me, I remembered a soul-thieving detail. An old fae law on marriage to mortals, one still upheld today, that instantly cursed my Seren-owned future. Even when our bind dissolved, the consequences of what I had done would not. She would walk free. But me? I was in deep trouble.

Taryn was now my property. I owned her mortal life. And, as such, I had effectively stolen property from Black Beak and would be fined—heavily. When we break the fifteen feet of freedom curse, Taryn would no longer be owned—by anyone. I will have paid for her freedom as her former master by taking on all her debt and punishments as a bride price to Black Beak.

My stomach sickened.

I couldn't let her know. Not yet. And definitely not within the five-day grace period. We had too much on the line right now with only fifteen days to break a curse. And if she broke our binds as a result, we would have no protection. *She* would have no protection against Black Beak. Mate of convenience she may be, but she was still my mate. I vowed to put her above all others.

Plus, it wasn't her fault. This was *my* mistake, *my* consequence to own.

All fae are taught the bonding laws as wee ones.

But, if I were honest, after a lifetime of being enslaved, knowing I perhaps had another decade or two more to endure instead of one year left was too soul crushing. I didn't want to talk about it with anyone, let alone with the person who gained all I had ever wanted. I couldn't stand being pitied, either. I had survived this long without feeling sorry for myself. No need to add emotions that unnecessarily complicated situations that couldn't be changed.

"The mud breaking your heart there, Finn?" Taryn asked, gently poking me in the back with her spear. I relaxed my face and leaned into the distraction. "You look like you're on the verge of crying a salt marsh to rival this cursed bog."

"Not a fan of the mud. Or hunting monsters in it."

"Maybe the Dobhar-chú relocated to a homier marsh," Taryn murmured.

I grunted in humor. "More marsh, less bog, with a misty mountain view, the dream of every Otter King."

"A patch of lawn for a garden and plenty of room for a bairn or two to romp around."

"With a wife in the kitchen who only cooks the finest meals for her mate."

"*Only* cooks?" I could hear the eye roll in Taryn's voice.

"Aye," I said with an impish smile. "Like all good otter wives. Take notes, love."

A ball of slimy mud splattered on my back and I held in the urge to reply with a rude gesture. The minx.

"With a husband," she added with false innocence, "who

scrubs all the mud from their clothes after a long day of hunting."

I twisted around to face her and let my gaze slowly drift down her body. "After his wife undresses before him first."

Her cheeks blushed scarlet, but her dark brown eyes threw daggers at me. "If he scrubs all the mud—"

"Oh, he will," I playfully cut in. "He will scrub every inch of clothing they own to watch his wife strip bare."

She arched a dark brow. "Been awhile for the Otter King, has it?"

"He simply never agreed to a mate bond in name only." I winked and turned around and took another mud-suctioned step. The anger at realizing I was right, that we had never included that language in our binding agreement, was practically rolling off her in billowing waves. And, because I apparently wanted another ball of mud to the back of my head, I added, "Otter wives are terrible at bargaining with Otter Kings. It's why they should *only* cook."

Another step.

And no mud ball retaliation.

Maybe the lass wasn't as predictable as I believed.

"You sure know a lot about the mating habits of Otter Kings for a Seren alley boy, Finny."

My lips twitched. "We were chums back in the day, Rynnie. Fun lad. Always told the best jokes, he did—"

A giant, heaping ball of slimy mud hit the back of my neck and splattered across the side of my face. I grimaced, followed by a gag. That mud stank worse than the witch's cottage. If we weren't hunting, I would make her take a dunk in this foul bog soup. But I played with the angry gust of wind that was my mate-of-convenience-who-cost-me-my-freedom and got her bite.

From behind, I could hear her growl while taking another mud-stuck step. Heaving an annoyed sigh, she asked, "So, if we find the Dobhar-chú of Fennel Marsh, our only plan is to somehow steal a tooth then flee. We can barely walk, how are we to flee?"

My plan was to kill the beast first. Made stealing a tooth and fleeing a might easier, aye? But I knew her humanity would clutch its pearls over the ethics of taking an "innocent" life for reasons the monster never chose. Fae didn't get their knickers in a twist over doing whatever was necessary to break curses or survive. Life was a bargain to us. Not like mortals, who would sacrifice themselves to prove that a monster had a beating heart like them. The foolish mortal would probably thank the creature while it crushed their bones, too. *Thank you, beast. I know you're good deep down inside, which I'll find out in another bite. You're just misunderstood.*

Feck. Me.

So, to avoid that insanity, I said what fae have told mortal girls since the sun began chasing the moon. "There's a legend that the Dobhar-chú will fall into a deep sleep only when a beautiful virgin maid sings him a lullaby."

She scoffed. "Why do males make a girl's virginity magical? The hubris to think he steals her magic from bedding her."

"Oh, love," I said with a cocky smile, "It's not to steal her magic. He pines to be the first to show her a male's."

Taryn's face fell in a you're-full-of-moon-shite look that encouraged me on.

51

"You see," I continued, my smile widening, "all other males will be compared to him afterward. And if he's good?"

"There it is," she muttered with a mild grimace of disgust.

"We are simple creatures, us males," I said, turning back around to keep walking. "We care only about the three F's. Food. A good fight. And fu—"

"Finn . . ."

"No, lass. Well, for sure, some males consider me their third F, but—"

"Finn Brannon!"

A predatory stillness fell over me. I heard every panicking warning in her tone and my animal instincts instantly clawed to the forefront. I followed the point of her spear to the reeds about twenty feet away. Two glinting red eyes glared back at me.

"Get behind me."

"Finn—"

"Get behind me now!" I shouted.

Thankfully she obeyed, moving as fast as she could to position at my back. The Dobhar-chú slowly rose from the murk, a giant creature twice as tall as me, with the head and body of an otter, the claws of a wolf, and with the small spine fins and tail of a water dragon. The beast cocked its head and blinked large red-glinting eyes at Taryn.

"It's so cute."

I shot Taryn an are-you-mad look over my shoulder. *Shite.* The creature had allure magic. "Do not trust your mortal instincts right now."

"I love otters," she said with a happy sigh, already under its

Dobhar-chú
Not an otter, but not *not* an otter.

thrall. "They're so darling, especially when they play with a rock in their adorable paws." Taryn began to demonstrate the motion with her hands and, if this were any other situation, I would throw my head back and laugh.

There was a chance Taryn would attack me if I attacked the Dobhar-chú. Unless . . .

Cursed stars, she was going to kill me. But the creature's allure intention was far more sinister.

With my spear lodged like a jousting lance in one arm, I twisted and grabbed Taryn by the chin and forced her to look in my eyes. "Mate," I said softly and magic drenched the air around our faces. The Dobhar-chú roared, the sound quaking down my body, its foul breath fluttering our hair. Her eyes snapped to the beast's and she giggled. I tightened my hold on her chin and forced her to look back at me. "Mate, you are scared of the Dobhar-chú but not afraid to fight." Her eyes rounded as the magic thickened with each word I spoke. "You want me to slay the beast and you will help me to do so."

"Finn," she said, her voice wobbling, the terror growing in her widening gaze. "I . . . I don't want to die."

The Dobhar-chú roared again and flapped its paws in the mud to slither-lope toward us.

"I'll protect you with my life, mate."

She nodded quickly and drew in a fortifying breath. "Let's thieve a tooth, Corbie."

"That's my Black Beak lass."

Twisting back to the beast, who was now roughly six- to eight-feet away, I raised my spear, relieved that I, not the Dobhar-chú, had control of Taryn's mind. The bog creature roared once more and a shudder scraped down my spine. Rows of sharp, jagged teeth lined its wide mouth.

I only had a second to shout, "Duck!" before a giant paw swung our way. I grabbed Taryn by her shirt and pushed her into the bog water. Sharp claws sailed over our heads. While its body was still in a swinging motion, I sprang up to a stand and jabbed my make-shift spear at the Dobhar-chú's chest. But the fur and skin were too thick.

My mind raced for an idea.

Another paw came at us and I dove into the water.

"Taryn," I rushed out. "Aim for its eyes. Or the soft area of its pa—RUN!"

The Dobhar-chú reared its head and lunged its sharp-toothed maw at us. The creature, I hoped, had a blind spot, similar to more reptilian bog creatures. Grabbing Taryn's hand, I dragged us as fast as possible toward the monster's side before its rough-furred head rose from the mud. The creature whirled on us with a swipe of a paw. I only had time to shove Taryn behind me and, with enough force, that she fell onto her arse and out of the strike zone.

But not me.

The pad of the Dobhar-chú's meaty paw slammed into my chest and torso, its claws scraping my side, just above the hip. My body flew a few yards in the air before splashing into the mud— but no more than fifteen feet from Taryn, thank the stars. A pained groan escaped my lips. But I couldn't lay here. Thankfully, I kept my grip on the spear. And, thankfully, the beast turned toward me and ignored Taryn completely. I rose on shaking legs, swearing when I saw blood blooming across my shirt.

My breath came quick. My limbs began to tremble, from adrenaline or venom or fear, I wasn't sure. I ran every morning, did pushups every evening. I could brawl like most alley lads. But I wasn't a warrior or monster hunter.

No, I was born in The Wilds and taken in by Caravan fae on the outskirts of Caledona Wood as a wee child after my clan was slaughtered in a raid. I grew up trained to con village folk from their coin at night markets only to be sold to Corbie when thirteen to release my foster mum from jail and to pay off my foster da's gambling debts. My life had never held much value other than for the profit of others. Even now, my value was the price of Taryn's freedom.

Still, I wasn't ready to die yet.

But I didn't know how to survive the next few minutes as the Dobhar-chú rounded on me. I lifted my spear, determined to pierce through its paw. Bared my teeth as the bog creature growled. Its claws swiped through the air.

> *Over the mountain, over the sea,*
> *Back where my heart is longing to be,*
> *Please let the light that shines on me*
> *Shine on the one I love.*

The Dobhar-chú stilled. And, at the same moment, both me and the bog monster swiveled our heads toward Taryn. She squared her shoulders and sang louder.

I see the moon; the moon sees me
Down through the leaves of the old oak tree.
Please let the light that shines on me
Shine on the one I love.

The creature let out a whimper, probably at the sound of Taryn's off-key voice. Aye, it was terrible. The beast and I could bond over this torment. But, right now, I wanted to wring her neck for believing my faerie tale and directing all of the Dobhar-chú's attention onto her.

"Run!" I mouthed, but she shook her head while continuing to sing. I gritted my teeth, then hissed as a sharp pain lanced up my side.

Taryn's eyes widened when the Otter King lowered to all fours, yawned, and blinked heavy lids.

Of all the shite stories to be true. I couldn't believe what I was seeing.

I hear the lark; the lark hears me,
Singing a song with a melody.
Please let the lark that sings for me
Sing for the one I love.

A snore rumbled from the beast before the last line was horribly belted into the air. Taryn faltered, unsure of what to do. I motioned for her to keep singing. The lass, bless her virgin stars, would never have a future as a bard. But she was officially a beautiful, mud-covered maid in a faerie tale.

With the Dobhar-chú sound asleep, I crept up to the beast and poked it with my spear. When it didn't wake, I inched closer, lifted its rubbery lips—forcing back the bile burning my throat—and began jiggling teeth to find a loose one. One tooth. Five teeth. Twenty teeth. Foul breath, the smell of a decomposing body, fluttered my hair with each snore, making me dry heave a couple of times. Occasionally I'd get a whiff of its sugar cookie scent mixing with the licorice of wild fennel. On the thirty-fourth tooth, I yanked, as I did all others, and fell back into the bog when it unexpectedly released.

I had a tooth.

Mother stars above, I had a tooth!

Quickly, I found my feet, wincing at the pain in my side and the bruises forming across my chest, and pushed my way through the sludge toward Taryn, holding up the tooth in triumph.

"You're bleeding," she said on a sharp gasp.

"I'm fine, love." I waved off her concern, then tucked the tooth into the pouch strapped to my belt. "Nothing that won't heal in time."

Weaving her fingers in mine, to keep us balanced, we took a step—and froze when marsh water splashed onto our faces. The Dobhar-chú was rolling onto its back, wolfy paws up into the air, then continued snoring. Taryn sputtered back a giggle. Brave was the person who could laugh in the face of death. And Taryn Hunt deserved a good laugh. We both did.

"Keep singing as we leave."

She dipped her head and continued.

I kiss a rose; the rose kisses me,
Fragrant as only a rose can be.
Please let the Rose that comforts me
Comfort the one I love.

One item recovered for the Crone. Two more left and we could go our separate ways.

Except, I was growing rather fond of her bitey company. Not of her singing, though. *Stars.*

Chapter Seven

TARYN HUNT

The bog marsh was at least a good hour behind us now. We were crusted in dry mud, swamp muck, and Finn was favoring his side while pretending nothing was wrong. But his skin was paler than usual and his breaths seemed more labored. My head felt strangely cloudy too, like it did right after that boy had used his coercion magic on me. I was unbelievably exhausted, though.

The moon hung in the sky above us and dusted the forest in silver. My eyes wandered over the wood and rested on a stretch of sparkling light through the underbrush.

"Is that a pond?" I asked Finn.

He turned toward where I pointed and squinted his eyes. "Aye, it appears so."

"Good. We could use a good scrub."

"There could be kelpies," he murmured.

I lifted a shoulder in a tired shrug. "There could be diseases in the bog marsh we wear too."

"Fair point."

We limped toward the twinkling water, both of us growing more desperate with each step. I was thirsty. So very, very thirsty. Hungry too. But I was used to working with little food.

At the bank, Finn placed a hand on my shoulder, a silent request to stay back, and then approached the pond. After a quick perusal, he determined it was safe to bathe in and to drink. Immediately, I dropped to my knees and cupped water with my hands, drinking until my belly felt fuller. Finn did the same. Falling stars, I didn't think I had ever been so thirsty in my entire life. I didn't even care that the water was warm and slightly bitter.

Standing back up, I turned my back to grant him privacy and directed, "You strip first and bathe. I'll wash your clothes once you're in the water then treat your wound."

Finn stepped into my path and my breath caught. "It's safer if we bathe together." His gaze darted around us before resting back onto me.

He was probably right. Still, I rolled my eyes. "Nice try, *Finny*."

A corner of his mouth lifted for a flutter of my racing heartbeat before he drew closer and whispered, "I don't need to try."

Those pale green eyes of his seemed to laugh at me.

"Your level of self-love is ridiculous," I whispered back, but didn't move away from his nearness.

"So, Rynnie—" his warm breath kissed my lips "—You're a virgin?"

I reared back, gritting my teeth. Really? He was now going to mock me? *Gods . . .*

No longer caring about his wounds, I gave that arsehole a good shove and stomped toward the water. Delighted when he grunted in pain.

First creepy skunks and now otter monsters. Well, not an otter. But not, *not* an otter. Midnight skies above, what a horribly embarrassing way to announce one's maidenhood too. And all to save the likes of Finn Brannon!

That annoying elf would never let me forget.

I was stuck with him too.

Finn straightened, but his smile remained crooked. Keeping his eyes squarely on mine, he unbuckled his belt and let it drop to the ground. Then he kicked off his boots and they tumbled to the water's edge. I followed his fingers as he toyed with a button on his breeches next, and shite. Heat flushed down my body and I blinked back the thoughts teasing my mind. I refused to play the blushing maiden for him, though. Crossing my arms over my chest, I arched an unimpressed brow. But he never removed his breeches. That irritating smirk still in place, he walked toward the pond, grabbing my belted tunic vest as he passed by, and . . . yanked me into the water with him.

I fell with a large splash and his laughter echoed off the water.

I sputtered and wildly wiped the droplets from my face.

Friends, I'm not sure if I would survive only fifteen feet of separation without murdering that stars-cursed, mischief-bent faerie boy in his sleep.

That faerie boy who was now taking my hands from where I sat in the shallows and pulling me to waist-deep waters. I didn't fight him though. The water felt wonderful, warm and perfect.

We sank to our necks, me glaring at him and him with a rascally grin aimed at me. And something inside of me broke. I snorted a laugh, then splashed water in his face. These past twenty-four hours were simply too much.

Will-ó-the-wisps, in hues of blue, green, and purple, danced over the rippling surface and wove through the fronds of several large ferns skirting the moonlit pond. It was magical and aggravatingly romantic. Finn's eyes trailed a few that spun by us. Then, as his gaze returned to study mine, he reached up to the messy knot of hair atop his head and pulled on a tie. Dark forest green strands tumbled down to the tip of his shoulders and thieving ravens bless me. Even with mud still splattered across his face, he was far too beautiful. A dangerous, predatory beauty that was quickly stealing the breath from my tightening lungs. The tiniest smile softened his lips right before he disappeared beneath the surface.

Stars, what was wrong with me?

I could not, would not look at Finn like all the other girls who crossed his path.

A current of water rippled around me and I rolled my eyes. I wasn't sure what Finn was doing, but I stood, not wanting to find out how he planned to test my patience next. I could sit in the shallows and finish bathing. I turned toward the bank when he popped up next to me, shaking the water droplets from his face and hair.

"Leaving so soon?"

He tossed his breeches toward the bank and my jaw fell open. The sodden garment landed with a wet thud. "Fiery suns destroy me now," I whispered under my breath. Then closed my eyes in a long blink when realizing he was probably eating up my reaction. To cover my mishap, I spun toward him with a ready quip on my tongue and stilled. He was trying to pull the shirt over his head, but the fabric was stuck to his wound and he hissed.

My stomach churned at the sight.

I couldn't be mad at him.

Not really.

He hadn't complained once about the pain I knew he was in. For a moment, I wondered if half of the smiles and jokes he tossed about were also to cover a different pain he wanted to hide. He wasn't from Seren, an observation that was growing more obvious by the minute.

A heavy sigh left me and I found myself saying, "Let me help you." I would see him shirtless to tend to his injury at some point this evening anyway.

My fingers tentatively lifted the torn shirt at his injured side and I peeled it back slowly. Finn lowered his hands to skim the pond's surface. His throat bobbed and he looked away. This was truly paining him and . . . was he ashamed?

"Finn—"

"No pity." His voice was tight. "No fussing"

I nodded my head.

Carefully, I pulled back more and more, unhooking threads caught in the lacerations. I wouldn't be able to treat his wounds properly until daylight. But, with the unnatural warmth of the water, this pond was most likely a mineral spring. The minerals would work as an antiseptic. He couldn't ask for better treatment right now. I gently touched a large bruise by his lower ribs. The clawed marks were, thankfully, not too deep or long. But they were angry. His chest rose and fell in quick breaths, his eyes pinched shut.

Remembering his warning, I dryly tossed out, "You can remove your shirt now and I'll pretend to swoon, but only this once."

His lips twitched. "I said no pity."

"Pity swoons are not pity but also not *not* pity."

Finn burst into laughter. It was a pleasant sound, deep and bright. "With riddling like that, lass, you might become more fae than me by week's end."

"Well, off with it, then, before I change my mind. I'm afraid of what will happen to you if a female doesn't fall at your feet at least once a day."

Another laugh left him. Then, playing into the not pity swoon command, his stare grew heated within a single blink as he licked his lips, and in an animalistic way that struck my trotting pulse into a run. He moved closer to me, close enough that I could feel his body's warmth. My eyes rose to his and . . . shite, I was in so much trouble. Light and shadows played across the planes of his cheeks, down his nose, his pale eyes appearing paler beneath the dark strands of his disheveled, shoulder-length hair. A canine softly bit down on his lower lip as he slowly, so, so slowly, lifted his shirt over his head.

The air grew thick around us.

I couldn't breathe.

Moon-touched droplets of water rolled down the hard lines

of his chest and down the ridged muscles of his stomach. Inky water lipped the V of his hips and my mouth parted. His body was bruised in spots and clawed and I was *still* panting. What would I do if he were unmarred? He tossed the partly shredded shirt to the bank beside his breeches. Swallowing thickly, my gaze trailed up to the curves of his upper arms and wide-set of his shoulders.

Finn's long fingers played with the floating end strands of my waist length braid. I wasn't sure why I let him, why I didn't step away, but he untied the ribbon and began unplaiting my hair until waves of muddy, dark brown strands cascaded down my arms and back. Those same fingers then caressed my cheek in feather-light touches before cradling my face with both hands.

Finn softly blinked. "The most important part of the legend, Taryn, wasn't that she was a virgin. Any maid would do, if so." He tilted my head, then lowered his mouth to almost brush against mine, whispering, "It was that she be beautiful. And, love," he paused, his voice growing rough, "your beauty is now proven legendary."

Then he kissed me. A sweet, chaste kiss so gentle, I could taste his heartbreak slow dance beside the moonlight spilling into my pulse. Why did this kiss feel so sad? I drew in a hiccuped breath. Tears gathered on my lashes. I didn't know why for him. But no one had ever said anything so kind to me before. I knew it wasn't just about him complimenting my looks or trying to make me swoon, but him telling me that I had held rare magic over his kind, the only reason we still lived.

He pulled back and brushed a tear on my cheek away with

his thumb. The heartbreak I felt in his kiss both softened and sharpened his gaze. Then he stepped backward, strands of my hair slipping through his fingers as he moved into deeper waters.

Our eyes remained locked.

Questions blurred back and forth between us. This wasn't real. I was confusing heartbreak for the pain I already knew he was in.

No pity. No fussing.

Cheating death made two people want to feel more alive, closer. A survivor's bond, that was all. Nothing more. Right? This boy kissed many girls. I had seen it with my own eyes and for years. I was just one more in his count.

A side of Finn's mouth hooked up in a familiar teasing smile. "You may have made a proper male of me, Rynnie, but seducing me at every turn is becoming a bit much. Give a lad a chance to catch his breath."

I scoffed, but grateful for the familiar back and forth. "Well, you've used up your one pity swoon, Finny. Don't expect another."

"No, love." That wicked grin of his grew wider. "The next one will be real."

"Name. Only."

"That wasn't a part of our sealed bargain, mate."

I clenched my jaw. "Mate of convenience."

"Aye." He shrugged. "But still my mate."

Always bartering. Always bargaining. Always a battle of wits. Rolling my eyes, I waved him off as I turned toward the shallows to finish scrubbing my clothes and hair, careful not to distance myself too far from him. Colliding with a completely naked Finn Brannon would be the end of me.

I brushed my thumb over the pair of ravens on my wrist and sighed.

This was going to be a long night.

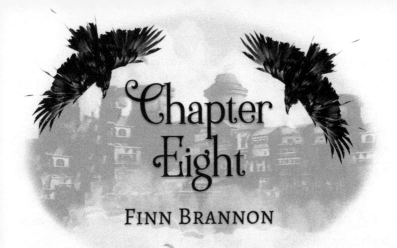

Chapter Eight

FINN BRANNON

The caw of a raven was the only warning I had as my eyes snapped open. The hair on my arms rose on end. We weren't alone. I lifted my ear to the wind, careful not to draw any watchful eyes to where Taryn and I lay, hidden beneath the ferns and underbrush around the pond.

A flutter of black wings in a nearby tree caught my darting gaze.

"Not here," the raven said, her black eye firmly fastened to mine. I tipped my head at the spy bird and lowered my head back onto my bed of moss. Why was the raven protecting us?

"Search the other side of the pond, S725."

With a caw, the bird alighted into the air and flew away.

We needed to move.

I rolled over to face Taryn and . . . my heart stuttered a beat. Last night, she was enchanted by the silver water and moonlight and I was completely under her spell. Even the will-ó-the-wisps were bewitched and gathered to dance in her presence. But right now, lying beside me? Long lashes dusted her cheeks, light olive skin softened in the dusky light, and her mouth. I blinked. Her mouth, only a few inches from mine, was slightly flushed from sleep. I had tasted those lips twice now. They were mine. Even after our mate bond was dissolved, I would tear down mountains if another male kissed her.

Finny boy, calm your pantaloons.

A bargain of convenience my mind agreed to but we were bound by ravens. A *real* mate bond before the fae. An ownership. And it was turning me into a territorial puppy dog for her. Aye, I could resist the magic, but I couldn't help but think of the Crone's comment.

My mortal mate.

What if Taryn was my True Mate?

What if the Crone only meant my bonded mate, knowing what we would do?

Stars, I could pull my hair out strand by strand right now. Mortals had the luxury of not having magic. The fae? We were ruled by a power so primal, so ancient, even the high fae, like me, behaved no better than animals when that wild magic took over.

More so for the wild fae.

Thirteen more days. She was a wound up, annoying, rival thief.

Not my wife.

Not my mate.

It was all in my head.

Anything I imagined on her part was *only* because mortals became elf struck. Even the singing challenged Taryn Hunt, no matter how much she fought the compelling magic all fae are born with. My biting, angry wind of a lass did a fair job of fighting it too.

Good.

Stealing kisses and becoming a mainlander's fantasy dalliance was easy.

Believing one was wanted, that one had family, only to be abandoned and kinless was not.

Especially when they would walk away free and I . . . I . . .

No, I wouldn't put myself in a position to feel those tearing emotions again, so help me.

"Taryn," I whispered, gently stroking her cheek. Feck. I needed to stop that. "Taryn Hunt." I tapped her face until her eyes fluttered open. Before she could snap at me, I lifted a finger to my lips and gestured with my head that we had company. Her doe eyes widened. Stars, those eyes.

Someone punch me in the otter wound!

"We need to move," I said more harshly than I meant to.

She nodded, not even fazed by my whispered, sweet nothings.

We got to our feet and crouched low, creeping to a copse of thicker trees. I peered around a large trunk and lifted my ear to the wind again. A hundred feet away, I spotted two males and a female, all elves. The raven flapped to another branch, leading them farther and farther away from us. Which baffled me. I peered down at my tattoos with wrinkled brows.

"Mercenaries?" Taryn asked beside me.

"Aye. Not sure if for us or that Black Beak runner."

"Shite . . ."

I turned to her, feeling a touch woozy. The corners of her mouth dipped into a frown. "No fussing. Let's go." Not giving her a chance to reply, I strode off in the opposite direction of our hunters.

Thunder rumbled across the rainy sky and I bit back a growl of my own.

I was a soggy, irritable cat. A sharp, hackled hiss was buried just beneath my shivering skin. If I looked at Taryn, I might just let it loose. The lass would hiss back too. She wouldn't be afraid to use her sharp claws on me either. I had the bruises from when she tackled me to prove it.

The rain had been pouring down on us for a couple of hours now. Cold, miserable drops that soaked my clothing and leached into my bones. The pain was fatiguing me too. The non-stop walking wasn't helping.

Not too far into our escape, Taryn had stopped for me to put on her long tunic vest to hide my blood-stained, shredded shirt should we encounter others frolicking through Caledona Wood in this stars shite storm. I bared my teeth in a reminder about no fussing. And then I put the damn thing on. It was a smart thing to do, despite my grumbles. But the fabric rubbed me through the rips.

What I would give for a warm fire and meal.

A raven perched in a branch a few paces ahead. I could see it's tagged talon and squinted my eyes. This was the third spy raven we had passed. Not a single one spoke, either to not alert Taryn, which would be strange, or because they were not on our side like S725.

"I'm about to pass out," Taryn murmured.

I peered over my shoulder and slowed my steps. Dark circles lined her eyes, droplets slipped down her face, and her teeth clacked. Looking away, she rubbed at her arms in a shiver. My skin felt clammy despite the rain and I wasn't sure if it was from infection or the pain.

"There's an inn up ahead," I mumbled.

Her eyes narrowed. "How many times have you been to the mainland?"

"That's your response? Not, 'Oh, Finn, you're the best mate a mortal girl could have. The most virile, handsome male in all Caledona Wood. Nay, the entire Kingdom of Carran. A strong, beautiful male who wants to sweep me off my feet, while bleeding out on the forest, and whisk me out of this. Gods. Damn. Rain. And put a roof over my head.'" I lowered to her face and gritted out, "Any other obvious questions? Or should we now skip ahead to the part where we start spouting sonnets like romantic fools? Then run off into the sunset to the inn where our passions flame hotter than the roaring fire we both desperately need but will never know because you can't take another step unless you know my. Stars. Blasted. Mainland. History?!"

"One more question—"

"Crone!" I shouted to the trees. "Take me! I'll make a handsome little skunk ornament!"

"—How do you plan on paying for a room?"

I made a sound somewhere between a sigh and scream. "A work for trade bargain."

73

Her mouth fell open to chide me, then clamped shut and pressed into a thin line.

That's right, lass. No fussing. I wasn't an ancient taking his last walk in the wood to remember the good times before passing on. This soggy, miserable cat could keep on hissing too.

Taryn looked away and violently shivered again.

Shite. Her lips were bluish from the cold. And I was wearing her warmest article of clothing. Shame crept up my neck and I clenched my fists. I could be a real arse sometimes.

Another shiver wracked her tiny frame and a growl settled low in my chest. A possessive sound that pounded beside my heart. And, before I realized what I was doing, I had stepped toward her, cupped her frozen face in my icy hands, and declared like a besotted lunatic, "I vowed to put you above all others. That includes my own needs. If I must labor the entire night for you to sleep by a warm fire, I will, lass, and without complaint."

Feck. Me. I was losing my luscious green-headed mind.

She stepped out from my touch. "Are you hot or cold, Finnan? Make up your mind."

"Finnan, is it?"

"*Finn* for typical murder eyes moods. *Finny* for those extra stabby feelings. And *Finnan* for when I'm ready to walk sixteen feet away and point a stick at your heart as you come flying back to me."

"That's beautiful, love."

"*Finnan*, I'm starting to feel like the bruised, plucked petals of a daisy you're not sure if you want to keep or discard."

"That was my bargain, Rynnie. To put you above all others."

I threw her a sly, baiting smile. "You made the same one. Feel free to perform grand gestures for me at any time."

Taryn shook her head and walked past me. "Two days and already I'm going mad."

"Mad in love," I shot back. "You are definitely touched in the head for me."

"That's you confusing your own feelings for yourself, Finny."

Ah, we had downgraded to Finny. I wasn't sure if I was sad or relieved.

The rest of the way to the inn was just as miserable as the rest. Rain, leaves blowing in the wind—and into our faces—and mud. I was tired of mud. One good thing about Seren: very little mud.

As we rounded a narrow deer trail, the inn came into view and it was just as dilapidated as I remembered. The rooms might leak, but there would be no more bugs than we found sleeping beneath the trees and, more importantly, it would be drier. It was near sunset. Lads from the nearby village were no doubt already in their cups. To keep our head low, I would knock on the back door.

"The Fiddling Duck," Taryn said, reading the lantern-lit sign slowly, then came to an abrupt stop. Music drifted from the tavern and I could see the wheels turning in her eyes after the skunks and Otter King. "If there's a real duck in there with a fiddle I'm going to riot."

"Not a real duck." I had to keep my lips from twitching. "But the Duck is also real."

"Finn Brannon, I am two breaths away from—"

"Come," I said simply and pulled her toward the tavern. The lass was barely wearing a shirt over her frame, the cotton was so thin. "Let's find out what can be done to earn room and board."

I guided her to the back service door and knocked. The door opened a few seconds later to a portly woman in her middle years. Her gaze landed on us and a scowl immediately pursed her lips.

"No charity." She started to shut the door, but I placed a hand on the hewn wood.

"Not charity, ma'am. We are hard workers and will earn our keep."

She released the door and fisted a hand on her hip. "What'll it be then, soup and ale or a room?"

"What jobs would cover both?"

"Duck!" she shouted over her shoulder. "Duck!"

Taryn shot me a glare. I bit the inside of my cheek to keep my face schooled as I stared straight ahead.

Duck Henrin appeared, wiping his hands on a towel before throwing it over his shoulder. The last ten years had aged him like it did for most mortals. Thick black hair was now sprinkled with gray and his once smooth skin wrinkled with the exhausted groans of the overworked.

"Looking to trade for a room?"

"Aye, sir. For one night."

The older man eyed Taryn, his gaze roaming down her drenched body. "She can work the back kitchen with me, washing dishes and cutting vegetables."

I felt a snarl forming at the way he was looking at my mate. Pulling her to my side, I wrapped both arms around her and rested my chin on her head. Stars, she was frigid. "My *wife* and I took a vow to only work together. It's an unbreakable bond, it is. Give us the job for two and we'll do them both—" I paused a beat, then emphasized "—*together*."

The woman huffed a sigh, waved a dismissive hand at us and waddled away. But the man kept a calculating eye on us.

"Have I seen you before, lad?"

"No, sir," I answered quickly, even though he had. Several times when my foster tribe's caravan would come through to set up a night market and perform in the neighboring village. But that was ten years ago. I had the earthen colorings more common of the wild fae, though.

"Start with chopping a half cord of wood. After that, see me in the kitchens to wash dishes."

"What is our payment?" I asked.

"We'll discuss when you're done."

I laughed darkly. Feeling my cold, shivering mate in my arms snapped something primal inside of me. "We bargain a fair deal up front. That is my first offer. If you refuse, I'll coerce you to give us the finest room and meal entirely at your expense. Might make you dance a jig or two atop one of your grand tables too. But that isn't fair to an *honest* gent like you, now is it?" Taryn's body stiffened. "By the looks of your inn, you are clearly in need of help, aye? So no more gobshiting."

The man grinned. I knew he would. Everything was for show with men like him. "I like you, elf. I thought you were too pretty and soft at first."

"Oh I'm pretty," I said with a replying grin, one that was part feral. "Now, what is your bargain?"

The man eyed Taryn a second then back to my bared teeth.

"Chop a half cord of wood then wash two basins of dishes and you can have a basement room, bowl of soup and cup of ale for each."

"And two bundles of wood for the room's stove."

"For that you'll need to chop a crate of vegetables each."

I narrowed my eyes. "Repeat your entire deal." I listened carefully as he went back through his bargain. A raven on the roof listened too and I cocked a brow. The man finished, I offered my hand and said, "Deal."

"Deal," the man said and grabbed my hand for a quick shake. "The chopping block is out that way." He pointed to a stack of logs. "Find me in the kitchens when finished." And with that, he shut the door in our face.

Taryn shoved me away. "You have coercion magic?"

I didn't have the energy for this conversation. Ignoring her question, I tugged on her hand to follow me. The raven on the roof leapt into the air and flew away. The spy ravens were really grating on my nerves.

"Finn," she growled.

"Later," I growled back.

Coercion wasn't a rare magic, but it also wasn't common. And I wasn't *him*.

At the log round, I removed my belt and Taryn's tunic vest, not wanting to aggravate my wound any more. She placed them under the inn's eave where I told her to wait until there was wood ready to stack. The first swing of the axe nearly brought me to my knees. But I picked up another log, gripped the handle, and swung again. Eventually I lost myself to a rhythm and splintered log after log as Taryn stacked them along the backside of the inn.

Rain continued to splatter on my face, drench my clothes. I knew my wound was bleeding again, though not much. But I wouldn't stop. Taryn was barely able to stand. I was in bad shape, but I was fae. Mortal bodies were weaker, more fragile, and she was beginning to look ill.

When finished, I forced myself into the kitchens, Taryn right behind me. We quickly set to work, her washing dishes while I chopped vegetables. She eventually joined me to finish the last crate. We worked in silence, as we did outside. I was counting down the seconds when I could strip and fall into the bed and not move.

"We're done, sir," I said to Duck.

He perused our work, then handed me a key. "Grab the bundles of wood yourself."

I nodded. "Fair enough. Send soup and ale to our room."

A few minutes later, with arms loaded with firewood, we stumbled into our room and dumped the bundles by the pot belly stove in the corner. Finding hay, kindling, and matches, I quickly built up a fire. The chill on my skin was so cold, it felt like I was burning. And if that was how I felt, I couldn't imagine what Taryn was experiencing.

Slowly, I stood from my crouch and, with a crooked smile, reached into the pouch at my belt and pulled out four potatoes. Taryn softly snorted as I placed them atop the cast iron to cook overnight. "Rule two doesn't exist on the mainland," I mumbled. Not that I adhered to that rule on Seren. I stole food all the time.

My eyes swept over the small, simple room. One that was, thankfully, not longer than fifteen feet in any one direction. A bed barely big enough for two took up one corner against the cob and timber wall. At the end sat an old chest with a busted lock. Near the pot belly stove rested a table and two chairs—and our meal. Steam wafted from the bowls and my mouth began to water.

Taryn closed her eyes and swayed, her teeth clacking.

That territorial puppy dog inside of me took over. I marched to the bed and stripped the blanket, pulled her in front of the stove, then held up the covers to grant her privacy. "Strip before you catch your death."

I expected her to argue, but she didn't. She didn't say a single word. The sodden, thin shirt hit the floor with a wet thwump, followed by her belt. A few seconds later, various herbs were tossed to the ground, followed by two carrots, cut in half, a couple radishes, and two kitchen linens.

"Seducing me with your thieving ways are you, Rynnie?"

She peered over her bare shoulder. "I only care about rule three right now."

I winked. "Sure you do, love."

Turning around, she removed her boots, stockings, and breeches, tossing them beside her shirt. I wrapped the blanket around her first, then wrapped my arms around her next. She leaned back on me, too tired to protest. This mortal needed more warmth and a low, protective growl rumbled from my chest. Lifting her up, I carried her to the bed, ignoring my screaming muscles, and set her down gently.

"I want to eat," she said, eyes closing.

"Just moving the table closer to the stove, is all." She nodded as I walked away. Took no time to rearrange the room, moving the table and chairs before the fire and dragging the heavy oak chest in front of the door. Then I picked her back up and placed her closest to the warmth. "The soup should have cooled down enough now."

Once more, she nodded her head, dug in—and moaned. How long since she'd had a proper meal? I'd wager she followed rule two and only feasted on the meager rations Black Beak offered daily—most did to avoid adding to their debts if caught. The dried fruit and nuts granted us for our travels wasn't much either.

The soup was watery, bland, but had a fair bit of vegetables and some chunks of beef too. At least, I hoped it was beef. Who knew in Caledona Wood. I watched her eat, taking in large spoonful after spoonful, and my heart sank.

"Lass, can you give the potatoes a quick turn?"

She lowered her spoon and twisted toward our future breakfast. I quickly poured some of my soup in her bowl, hoping the crackling fire hid the sloshing sound, then lifted a spoon to my mouth with a loud slurp as she turned. Taryn didn't bat an eye at me or notice the added food in her bowl. She just picked up her spoon and continued eating with eyes half-closed. Afterward, she downed her cup of ale, then lowered her head to the table.

"Come, you wee thing," I murmured, picking her up again. My arms shook after hours of cutting wood. Pain lanced up my side. But I focused all my remaining energy on her. In a few steps,

I deposited the tiny, feisty lass on the bed. Taryn's head hit the pillow and she groaned, curling up.

Taryn Hunt was going to be the death of me. Two days and already war drums beat in my chest for this girl. The bonds demanded I battle to provide for and protect my mate—the root magic and nature of my kind too—no matter how I felt about her or the consequences in owning her. Moon above, she was about as fun as being dumped into a bag of hissing opossums some moments and, in others, like floating through the star-flecked sky.

Though, I was increasingly becoming fond of hissing opossums.

She was adorable when all fired up.

There were moments on the trail, while we were swapping guild stories before the rain washed away my chipper mood, that her playful laughter and sharp wit stole my breath. I have never known a mortal girl like her before—soft yet unyielding, clever and cleverly funny.

I turned away to add more wood to the stove. Then I stripped, laying our clothes over the chairs and table and our boots beside the fire. I placed the carrots, radishes, and herbs on the table too.

My bare skin prickled in the mixture of heat and chill. Stars, I could sleep for days. Gently, I crawled into bed beside my mate and positioned the blanket to cover us both. Then I wrapped my arm around Taryn and pulled her in close to share our body heat. She could bite my head off in the morning . . . when she was warm. Right now, she was still frigid and shivering in her sleep.

The last thing I remembered before passing out myself was the perfect feel of her body pressed to mine.

Chapter Nine

TARYN HUNT

My eyes fluttered open in the dim light. But they wanted to remain shut. I sank back into the cloud that was my bed compared to the forest floor and my cot at Beggar's Hole. A soft moan sighed from my lips as I rolled over and buried myself into a wall of soft, smooth warmth. So, so warm. Smelled good too. Spring rain, mossy trees, cinnamon. Arms cradled me closer; a face nuzzled into my hair.

My eyes snapped open.

That was a body holding me. I had burrowed into a muscular chest—my heart stopped beating.

Oh my stars!

Finn was naked. I was naked. *We were naked.*

I started to move and Finn tightened his hold.

"No," he murmured into my hair.

My pulse began thrumming wildly. "We're undressed," I whisper squeaked.

83

"For survival, love, nothing more."

"We're clearly alive."

He smiled into my hair, then adjusted to pull me in even closer. And because I was weak, I didn't resist. He was so warm and the bed was so soft and my body ached all over and he smelled so good. But we couldn't cross this line. He may not have agreed to a marriage in name only, but I would *not* be another one of his conquests.

"Finn—"

"Taryn," he mumbled in a half groan. A hand patted my face. "Shhh. You're not done sleeping."

I rolled my eyes. "You're an eejit."

"Mmm," he answered.

Fire ignited in my blood and fevered across my skin at the breathy, husky sound of his hush-now, sleepy-time moan. I should shove him away, but his steady breaths feathered my hair not even a minute later.

The next time I woke, it was to an empty bed. I gathered the blankets to cover my chest and slowly rose to peer around the room. Finn sat at the table by the fire, his profile to me, clothed in only his breeches. He had tied up his hair into a messy knot again. The muscles in his arms softly flexed as he fidgeted with the Dobhar-chú's tooth in his fingers. My eyes trailed down the lines of his broad shoulders, down his chest, down his stomach. He was mesmerizing. And that body held mine all night.

There was something seriously wrong with me.

No, I needed to steel myself against his flirtatious charms . . . and his masculine beauty. *Stars.*

"What time is it?" I asked to alert him that I was awake.

Finn glanced in my direction, not quite meeting my eyes. A slight scowl between his brows deepened. "Mid-morning." He returned his attention back onto the tooth. "I'll step out of the room so you can dress."

Without waiting for a reply, he scooted the chest away from the door and disappeared into the hallway, shirtless and barefoot.

I didn't know how to take his withdrawn, brisk demeanor. Pushing it from my mind, I tiptoed from the bed, the blanket wrapped around me, fetched my clothes and dressed quickly. While buckling my belt, I strode to the door and yanked it open. Finn nearly fell inside. Had he been leaning his forehead on the door?

Our gazes touched. The scowl between his brows deepened even more.

Grabbing his arm, I pulled him inside and shut the door. "What's wrong with you? Besides the obvious?"

"We'll need to stowaway on the ferry," he answered, completely ignoring my jab.

I crossed my arms over my chest. "You're in a mood over thieving a ride to Seren? And why are we returning to Seren?"

His throat bobbed. "The Amulet of Oisín—"

"You're a broody rain cloud over the amulet? No, I don't think so." A muscle jumped along his jaw. "Spit it out, Finny, or I'll only call you Finnan and distance myself as many times as it takes for some good sense to get knocked into you."

A ghost of a smile touched his lips, but it disappeared within a breath. Then he gently walked me up against the door and caged me in between his arms. My heart stopped beating. I wasn't sure if I were breathing either. Was he about to kiss me again? Would I push him away if he did?

"Taryn," he whispered. "We were trailed by spy ravens yesterday. Not sure if it was the same one or four different ravens."

I groaned, pissed that I entertained a kiss and pissed that he was being dramatic over nothing. "We're on a job, of course there are spy ravens. There's *always* spy ravens."

"Aye, but one protected us yesterday. At the pond. S725."

My eyes widened. "That's a Black Beak tag."

"S725 looked right at me, told the three mercenaries 'not here,' then led them away."

"That . . . doesn't make sense."

"Unless you're not the target. They could still be looking for the runner."

My shoulders relaxed.

"But it's only a matter of time. We need to show our mate bond to Primry Green."

My faced scrunched up. "Why Prim when it's Black Beak on the hunt?"

He pressed his forehead to mine and closed his eyes. "I stole from Black Beak the moment I bound myself to you and you to me. You are mine, Taryn Hunt. The Kingdom of Carran will only recognize you as belonging to me and no other, not even Black Beak."

A sudden gust of fury punched me in the gut. "You . . . *own* me?"

He flinched. But he didn't answer.

"Did you trick me? Is this mate bond all a trick?"

"No." His throat bobbed and he drew in a shaky breath. "I didn't remember this fae law in marrying a human until you were almost done with your vow. I'll swear on anything just don't do something rash."

I would make him swear, but I remembered the terrified way he had looked at me. The way he had paled. Even now, I could tell he was tormented by this so-called law. A sigh loosened from my tightening chest. He was telling the truth, but I couldn't make sense of what he was telling me.

Carran was originally fae lands. Humans populated most of our kingdom now. I didn't know much about the fae or human laws, though, only the three guild rules I was required to live by. Didn't know much about marriage laws either, fae or mortal. Why would I?

"So . . ." My furious mind skidded to an abrupt stop. "I'm now a Corbie until we break our curse?"

"You'll live at Prim with me until our bond dissolve."

He opened his mouth as if to say more, then closed it. But I knew what he didn't say.

I would live with him at Prim unless I broke our bonds.

Black Beak would not let this go unpunished. Already, I felt my heart grinding to dust at knowing Corvus would add more debt to my indentured account to work off once Finn and I could go our separate ways, and it wouldn't be a small sum either. I failed the job *and* married a rival guild's thief who now owned me instead of him. No, I wouldn't break our bonds. But . . .

"Three years left," I whispered in confession, biting back the angry tears. "Catching the witch's ring would have reduced it to one. This curse, our temporary mate bond, your *ownership* has cost me my dream to open an apothecary shop."

Finn lowered a hand to caress my cheek, his pale eyes darkening. "Promise me, love," he whispered back. "Promise me you'll open that apothecary shop the moment you're free."

"Is this a bargain?" I asked, my lips trembling. Shite, I would not break down.

"Aye, make this bargain with me."

"Why do you even care?"

His hand cupped my face as he stepped in closer. "The witch's ring would have freed me from Corbie. Lass, I have been owned since I was four years old." My breath caught. "Owned and traded away as an Outsider slave by my Traveler blood foster parents." His thumb caressed the corner of my lip. "I don't want to own you, Taryn. I *only* want to own myself."

I blinked back the heaviness settling on me. "I . . . I didn't kno—"

"No pity, love. No fussing. I'm twenty-three, been thieving my whole life, and accepted this fate long ago."

Why he evaded my questions about his history with the mainland now made sense. My soul was cracking. "I'll promise you, Finnan Ó Brannon, but only if you promise to claim something you want the moment you're free too. It's only fair."

The heartbreak I noticed at the pond returned to his eyes and softened the curve of his lips. "I promise you, Taryn Hunt."

"Then I promise, too. Now," I said, placing my hands on his chest and pushing him back. "Let me look at your wound before our next Crone's quest."

I needed a distraction.

I needed a job to occupy my mind instead of this grief.

And so did he.

Grabbing Finn's hand, I tugged him toward the bed and gestured for him to sit on the edge. Finn arched a single humored brow, a flirty twist to his lips—but I knew it was all a farse. He smiled away his pain while I openly festered.

I fetched the linens, parsley, and sage I pilfered from the kitchen last night, then knelt before him and studied the angry skin and areas where the wound was still open. It didn't look infected, thank the falling stars. The last thing I wanted was to lug around this lump of a faerie while he fever babbled bargains or riddles with the rocks he kicked on the trail.

Bruises dotted above the claw injury along his ribs. A large bruise also swelled on his lower left pectoral. His eyes were fastened to my face the entire time I inspected his torso. The intensity of his stare blushed in my veins.

Pretending to inspect a bruise, I poked at the purpled skin. "Does that hurt?"

He grimaced.

"How about here?" I poked at another bruise. He winced and I bit back a smile. "And here?"

"This one pains me terribly." He pointed to a bruise low on his hips, at his pants line. "I can lower my breeches, if you need to inspect me more closely."

Our eyes locked. The smug tilt of his lips dared me to poke another bruise. He knew, probably the whole time. But, friends, I didn't regret making him suffer, not even a little. From the mischievous glint in his eyes, he didn't regret that he let me either.

The parsley and sage were limp and a little dry around the edges. They would still work, though. I stripped the leaves from the stems and began grinding them between the palms of my hands. Without a mortar and pestle, this would have to do.

"The parsley," I said, dabbing the slimy hand-made poultice onto the lacerations, "helps to stop the bleeding. Sage—" I plopped a hefty dab of green on his skin "—is a natural anti-inflammatory." I wiped my hands on a stolen linen, then tore it and the second one into long strips. "Lift your arms." He obeyed, watching me closely as I wrapped the material around his waist to cover the injury. "If I had garlic, honey, comfrey, and other ingredients, I would make a far better poultice for you."

A side of his mouth lifted. "Deal."

"Wait. I didn't—"

Finn started laughing.

"You know what, Finny?" I stood and placed a hand on my hip. "I've decided you must swear your truth after all."

His humor fell. "Why?"

I grinned, like a purring cat who had finally cornered a mouse. In a couple of steps, I reached an overnight baked potato on the table and his brows shot up. Why a potato? I didn't know. He made me so stars cursed flustered, I grabbed a potato. Not a piece of iron. Not the Dobhar-chú's tooth. A fecking potato. Well, I was already invested in this game of wit we were playing.

Lifting my chin, I demanded, "Swear on this potato that, as your thieving partner, you will not trick me into deals or riddle me into insanity."

Finn threw his head back with a loud laugh. "I can't believe you're asking me to swear away the beating heart of my fae soul on a stolen cooked potato." He laughed again, ignoring my angry eyebrows and murder eyes. Then, just when I thought he might take me seriously, he snatched the potato from my hand and took a large bite. "No deal."

I narrowed my eyes. "Then what will you swear on?"

A sensual smile settled on his lips. "I swear on a kiss that, as your thieving partner, I will not trick you into any deals."

"Or riddle me into insanity."

"Oh, love," he crooned, wrapping his arms around my waist and pressing his mouth softly to my stomach, "that requires far more than a kiss."

Horror shot through me. "You want my first child?"

"What?!" Finn looked up at me equally as horrified. "That was a mild riddle, Taryn. You should not be experiencing barter-ing-away-my-first-born-child level of insanity."

"Then why did you kiss my stomach?"

"You thought—" Finn cut himself off and fell into another loud laugh. "Oh, Rynnie, my sweet, naive, beautiful virgin faerie tale maid, my adorable wee otter wife, I swear on a cooked potato that I will not trick you into giving up your first-born child."

"Or any child of mine." At this point, I might as well roll with it.

He laughed again. "Or any child of yours."

Stars, his laugh. I could listen to him laugh all day and all night.

"Deal," I said quickly, then stepped out of his embrace. "Let's go. We have a ferry to sneak onto."

If I spent any longer in this room, I would either kiss him to seal his bargain—blaming it entirely on the riddles that were, obviously, driving me to insanity. Or, I would beat him with the remaining cooked potatoes. And I was looking forward to a nice breakfast for once.

A few minutes later, we were fully dressed, had our spare food tucked away, and left The Fiddling Duck behind us.

Chapter Ten

TARYN HUNT

Steam hissed into the air from the newly arriving ferry. The The train station and ferry dock bustled with mainlanders from all over. Caledona Wood, the last of the wild faerie forests in Carran, stretched the western side of our map. And by magic and various steam mechanics, Seren floated high above, just shy of kissing the borders of two other kingdoms.

A train whistle blew and I nearly jumped out of my skin. Passengers stepped onto the steam engine to leave Caledona Wood, the preferred method of travel for those in the large eastern cities.

"Love," Finn said to the target beside us, one I'd gander was just barely twenty. "You dropped your pocket watch."

The girl peered up at Finn and stilled. His lips curved into a flirty smile. A blush warmed her skin and I rolled my eyes. The two of us had pickpocketed several mainlanders as an offering to Corbie, hopefully to soften the blow. Or to trade for coin should we need to run. But this target had two ferry tickets sticking out from the front pocket of her travel dress. Stealing these was easier than stowing away.

"This is yours, aye?" he asked the young woman and she seemed to snap out of her elf struck spell. "A handsome piece. Family heirloom, is it?"

"Yes, an irreplaceable one."

Well, wasn't she a bright one? Was there such a thing as a replaceable family heirloom?

The girl gently plucked the watch from Finn's palm, sliding her fingers down his before pulling her hand away. "I noticed you earlier. By the train."

"I noticed you too." The sudden smoky tone of Finn's voice grated on me.

The girl pushed back her shoulders to draw attention to her low-cut bodice and the corners of Finn's mouth melted into sensual lines. Something inside of me flipped at his response. A boiling emotion that was building the more her eyes took him in slowly.

"How can I repay you?" she asked in a breathy voice.

Stars, she was still elf struck. What was wrong with all these mainlander girls? Not enough elves in the eastern cities? My mind paused on that for a second. Maybe there really wasn't. That would explain so much of the behavior on Seren.

When Finn didn't reply, she added with a flutter of her lashes, "Anything you desire."

"Anything?"

Mainlanders, gather close and listen to my soul-weary wisdom after spending three blissful days—truly the most blissful of my entire life—attached to an obnoxious, irritating faerie who bargains in his sleep. Don't *ever* say "anything" to a fae for *any* reason. Unless you really don't care about your happiness. Or the skin on your body. Maybe your left eyeball. Especially if you're partial to your sanity.

The girl bit back a demure smile and, like an eejit, said, "Anything."

Finn stepped in closer, gently resting his fingers on her waist. "There's two things I want, lass. Maybe you could help me out." His hand slid down her hip and I ground my teeth.

If I had to watch a moment more of this, I would walk fifteen feet and one-half inch from Finn and make sure this lady was between us when we collided.

"Ye all right, Frank?" I cut in, bumping into the girl, as if losing my balance after a hurried traveler bumped into me. "Watch it, mate!" I shouted behind me for extra effect. Finn lifted the tickets as she turned to me in surprise. Keeping my eyes on Finn, I continued, "Ye never go after girls just barely out of knee dresses and pigtails." I practically growled a smile at the young woman. "No offense, love. Frank gets confused on the third day of the week every week, he does."

Finn's brows shot up and he mouthed "Frank?" in disbelieving humor while the girl's head was still turned, but quickly smoothed his features when she faced him once more.

"Aye, I'm a fluffy bunny for the mature lasses, it's true," he said to the poor mainlander. "They get their claws on my young, tender but handsomely virile and energetic flesh and I'm a helpless lad, each and every time." He turned to me with a sweet, in-

Fluffy Bunny

How the mature lasses see Finn.

nocent smile and pretended to claw the air with a hand. "Isn't that right, my wee but much, much older forest cat?"

The girl's mouth fell open in shock as she studied me, and I smirked.

"I eat two cans of sardines and rub my skin with snail juice every day. An anti-aging ritual I learned from a witch on Seren, I did." The girl's eyes rounded even more. "Not even Frank knows how old I really am."

"Don't tell me, my feisty skunk ornament." Finn wagged a finger at me and my lips twitched. "It will ruin the fantasy and you know how much I enjoy our fantasies."

"Oh I do, Frank. I do."

"Pardon me," the girl said quickly, angling away from us. "Thank you, er, Frank, for returning my pocket watch."

"Anytime, love," Finn said with a dramatic dip of his head.

We watched her push through the crowd, then I turned and punched his arm.

"Jealous, Rynnie?"

I was ready to punch that smug grin off his face next.

"Keep fantasizing, *Frank*." I pulled a look of disgust. "A fluffy bunny for the mature lasses? Energetic flesh? Does your self-love have no shame?"

Finn's answering grin was so rascally, I groaned. But with a smile.

I had to admit, albeit begrudgingly, that his arrogant arse was growing on me. His laugh, his teasing ways and sharp wit, how his eyes softened while watching me when he thought I didn't notice. How he grew protective at times. I shouldn't want his protection either. I had been living on the streets for years. But he chopped wood in the pouring rain while injured then made sure I was warm and fed before caring for himself. My own Da hadn't treated me with the same care. How could I *not* be confused?

"Come, my feisty forest cat." He pawed at me, grinning wider when I groaned—again. "Our ship sails soon."

We boarded the ferry with our meager belongings and slumped onto our stolen seats in coach. Passengers stared at our mud-stained, bedraggled state and whispered to one another. *Yeah, the unbathed peasants in ripped clothing older than your money sit among your class. Piss off.* Finn took my hand in his and gently squeezed. Just that small gesture calmed my embarrassment some and eased my spinning nerves.

The ferry pushed off the dock with a jolt. Steam curled across the windows. A clank popped in my ears and then we were moving, slowly rising above the mainland on a steam-powered lift. The world below grew smaller and smaller. Finn leaned over, resting his chin on my shoulder, to see out the window. His cheek brushed mine and I had to focus on breathing.

"We were there," he said softly, pointing over Caledona Wood in the far distance. "A piece of me is still there."

I turned toward him and he eased back so our eyes could meet. "What was it like growing up in The Wilds?"

"The stars for a roof, the wind for my breath, and the earth in my heartbeat." A sad smile ghosted his lips. "I was little when my clan was slaughtered, but I remember the elemental magic. The connection to nature stayed with me for years after I lost my family, my home."

His clan was *slaughtered*? Stars above, my heart. I was about to comment, but then I remembered: no pity. My thumb caressed the back of his fingers and his gaze focused on my touch. "Is Finnan Ó Brannon your birth name or one the Caravan fae gave you?"

Humor pulled at his mouth. "Are you asking for my True Name, lass?"

I rolled my eyes in reply. He was so good at twisting my words to not answer a question.

The goddess Danu whispered a faerie's True Name in their ear at birth. Not even a mother knew her faerie child's True Name. If discovered, the faerie could be commanded to do *anything* and they would have no choice but to obey. Coercion magic for those immune to coercion magic.

Clearly I wasn't asking about his True Name, the eejit.

We fell silent and I continued to watch the world beneath my feet disappear into the rolling clouds. Seren had a tall, thick window wall that fenced the entire perimeter of the island. Sometimes I liked to sit at the edge of Beggar's Hole to watch the sun fall through the clouds. The pinks, oranges, gold, lavender were breathtaking.

The stars for a roof . . .

A light buzzing sensation trickled in my head. I drew in a deep breath and exhaled slowly. My mind began floating in a way I had felt before, but I couldn't remember how or why. I didn't care, though. I only cared about indulging in whatever made me happy, every fantasy, every want—

Finn's eyes snapped to mine. Anger thundered in his gaze. Why was he pissed with me? Before I could ask him, he cradled my face and drew me close.

"Mate," he spoke across my lips in reply.

Heady pleasure, unlike any other, rippled down my body with just that one word. *Mate*. Besides my freedom, I possessed no greater fantasy than him, my husband of convenience. No greater desire. Even now, I couldn't stop drinking in his beauty. I could drown in his smiles, his laughter, his teasing wit, the gentle feel of his hands on my skin. A thief's touch. No one had cared for me the way he had. No one had even come close to making me feel like I mattered.

"Steal a thousand kisses from my lips, Finnan. Then steal a thousand more." My fingers traced along the edge of his ear to the point and he shuddered. "Make my heart your next catch."

"Taryn . . ." His voice cracked; his throat bobbed. He closed his eyes in a long blink, then said, "You will resist the coercion magic on the ferry. It is not allowed to touch your mortal mind."

I blinked back sudden confusion. What was he talking about? And what was I just doing? I pulled away, my head feeling thick. A small headache formed at my temples, my mouth growing dry. Why did my skin feel so tight and hot? Finn wouldn't meet my eyes, either. Did I do something?

"You've always ridden in the hold, aye?" he asked, eyes lowered to the hands curling in his lap.

I nodded. That's where the fae and Seren natives were bussed to when traveling to the mainland and back. Though, I had only been to the mainland one other time. His narrowed eyes skimmed over the passengers. A muscle jumped along his jaw, the scowl between his brows growing deeper.

"What's going on?" I whispered.

The fingers of his hand played with the tip of my braid. He appeared lost for an answer. But why? Still not looking at me, he eventually murmured, "Magic not meant for you, love."

My heart stopped. This feeling. I remembered this thick, groggy feeling. "Did you just use coercion magic on me?" I hissed under my breath.

"Aye—"

"—How dare you!"

Finn leaned in and gritted out, "I was protecting you, not using you. There's a difference, *mate*." He gestured at all the people around us who smiled too wide, eyes too bright, their skin flushed with excitement.

"Shite on a cracker," I muttered under my breath in complete horror. I had always figured the tourists saw us beggars and thieves as part of the illusionist fun of Seren instead of real. And yet, no matter what happened on the island, they returned. "Do you think they're coerced to forget certain parts of their time on Seren, too, before returning to the mainland? How else could no harm be done to one's reputation, aye?"

That muscle along his jaw continued to tick. "Do you remember what you said to me before your mind woke?" The sharp-edged tone of his voice rose the hair on my arms.

"Is that why you're so worked up right now?"

He turned in his seat so quickly, I reared back. "Taryn..." His chest was rising and falling fast, the heat in his eyes burning my skin where his gaze touched me. "Do you remember anything? A word, a feeling, a confession, a command?"

I searched my mind but couldn't recall anything specific. "The last we spoke was of your name."

Pain cracked across his fury-tightened features. Chills prickled down my spine. A second later, a smile fluttered on his lips, one I would believe was playful if not for the crushed look in his eyes.

"Aye, love." His voice was soft. "You were trying to riddle out my True Name." He leaned in close, his smile growing wider. "And you never will, my wee unicorn beam of sunshine."

"What is it with you and unicorn sunshine?" I scoffed.

"When you discover my True Name, lass, I'll tell you."

My eyes rounded. "Unicorn sunshine is real?" He opened his mouth to reply and I quickly put my finger to his lips. "Don't ruin it with a not *not* clause. Let me believe this one faerie tale."

Finn laughed, though his eyes remained guarded, and my heart trilled a beat. By the stars, he was beautiful. Looking away, I daintily cleared my throat. The last thing I needed was for Finn to notice my staring. There was no escaping him and I suffered his flirtatious vanity enough.

I studied our entwining fingers as he pulled my hand to his lap. And, for a single flutter of my pulse, I felt the heartbreaking loss of him. As if when we stepped onto Seren, we would go our separate ways.

Twelve more days . . .

Chapter Eleven

FINN BRANNON

Shoppers crowded the entire length of Crescent Street. A perfect day to work the market, if I weren't about to have my pretty eyes pecked out by guild master for stealing a Black Beak from Corvus.

Steal a thousand kisses from my lips, Finnan.

Heat settled low, a swelling ache that made every step more miserable than the last. I was her stars damned *fantasy*. Of all the indulgences she could claim, she desired me. Not tables full of food. A warm roof over her head. Feck, even a new change of clothes. No, it was *me*.

Make my heart your next catch.

Those last six words tossed me off the ferry boat to plummet through a twilight sky of conflicted emotions. A high-speed fall that ripped the air from my lungs.

The coercion magic was intense. It fizzled down my body and tasted of copper on my tongue.

There was never any doubt in my mind that the tourists were under a spell. But the magic's bargain? I believed it mild, more carefree. A wee dancing jig of the mind to forget about one's worries, a happy escape to indulge in fantasies without harm to one's reputation.

The bargain fascinated me. Mortals willingly traveled to Seren knowing they would not remember certain aspects of their trip, if Taryn were any indicator. An island natively populated by far more fae than humans too. Fae needed to be commanded by their True Name for coercion magic to work between faeries.

"Finn!" a familiar voice called out. I turned to Kalen, who swaggered up to me with an arched brow at my mate. "Taryn Hunt, always a displeasure to see your rival thieving arse."

She lifted a rude gesture. "Kalen Kelly, go choke on rotten stardust."

Kalen jerked unruly midnight strands from his dark blue eyes. "A whole week I wept from boredom while you galivanted old haunts without me, Finn. Let's find trouble now, aye?" He grabbed my arm, turning me away from Taryn. "Crawl back into your Hole, Black Beak."

A quiet growl rumbled in my chest at the barest thought of separation from my mate.

Calm down you slobbering puppy dog.

Thieving stars, I needed to get a better grip on myself. Turning into an animal whenever someone threatened to take Taryn from me was ridiculous. And, yet, I knew it wasn't just our mate bond riddling my head. I was falling for Taryn Hunt. The growing obsession was different than the mate bond. I found myself craving the warm feeling thrumming in my chest. The past few days were some of the happiest of my life. Ribbing her, going on adventures with her, sleeping beneath the stars of Caledona Wood beside her.

Kissing her in a moonlit pond.

Waking to her sleep-softened face.

Unplaiting her dark hair to feel the silky strands slip through my fingers.

I wanted to catch her heart—I didn't care how short her mortal life was compared to mine. In another lifetime, we could have been happy together. Even if we were soulmates, as the Crone *possibly* suggested, this life was owned.

Kalen's grip tightened on my arm, a pressure that snapped me back into awareness. Stars, I was daydreaming about Taryn. Panic touched my pulse. The crowds were too thick. Becoming separated was a real possibility here, especially with Kalen bent on causing mischief. So, to ensure Taryn and I didn't provide a public flying demonstration, I reached for my lass and she gripped my hand just as Kalen tried to yank me away. But I held firm. My friend's dark brows pinched together.

"Kal, Pots Alley in twenty. We're in a bind, if you catch my drift."

"Shite . . ." Kalen breathed, looking at our clasped hands. "With *her*?"

"Twenty minutes, Kal, yeah?"

"Aye, I'll see you there."

The lad slid into the crowd and disappeared within seconds. I dropped Taryn's hand and gestured with my head for her to follow. We wove across Crescent Street, between vendor carts, through the strip of trees that separated the faerie market from the rest of Seren's pleasures. A few minutes later, we fell into the shadows of the main alley leading to Primry Green. A block down, I hung a left and picked up the pace toward Pots Alley, so named for the giant boiler pots in the adjoining factory. Steam hissed from a few pipes along the brick building and billowed around our bodies. A perfect place to hide one's voice and identity.

Taryn leaned up against the brick wall and picked at the mud beneath her nails. I paced in front of her, anxious for Kalen's arrival. We didn't have to wait long.

"Before we speak," I said to Kalen, "promise me you won't share a single word of our conversation."

Kal studied Taryn a moment, then shook my hand in agreement. "What kind of bind do you have with Miss Black Beak here?"

Taryn ignored him.

"A bind we have and a bind we're in, mate."

Gently, I took Taryn's hand and exposed her wrist, placing mine beside hers.

Kalen swore and closed his eyes in a long, nervous blink. His skin ashened to a sickly hue. "She's stolen goods now, she is. What the feck did you do, Finn?"

I told him everything, from the witch's cottage, our curse, marrying to escape hunters and to grant us time, facing off with the Dobhar-chú, and how a Black Beak spy raven helped us.

"Twelve days left . . ." Kalen whistled, running a hand

through his rumpled hair.

"The Amulet of Oisín," I said to him, "ever heard of it?"

"Oisín, the faerie king of Tír na nÓg?"

"Where?" Taryn cut in, eyes wide. "Is that far from here?"

"Aye, love," Kalen said with smirk. "Beyond our reach, it is."

"The Land of Youth," I explained. "The faerie Otherworld."

"An interesting choice, Oisín," Kalen continued, ignoring Taryn's horrified look. "The Maiden is clearly riddling you."

I narrowed my eyes. "How so?"

"Finn MacCool was Oisín's father, aye?"

"I'm an eejit," I muttered. Why hadn't I thought of that until now? Before Taryn could agree about my idiocy, I shared, "Finn is a legendary hunter-warrior who led the great Fianna. Our word for war band. A handsome devil he was too." I ended with a wink and she groaned.

"Now he's riddling you, Black Beak," Kalen said with a laugh. "Finn means 'handsome' in our fae tongue."

"Of course, it does," she grumbled, then pushed off the wall and settled beside me. "So, the Maiden wants you to find an amulet from the Land of Youth that belonged to the son of Finn?" She paused a moment, then asked, "What does Oisín mean in your tongue?"

Kal's eyes snapped to mine.

"Fianna!" we said at the same time.

"Stars feck me," I groaned.

Lady Fianna Winslow. The ruby necklace dangling happily on her well-endowed cleavage.

Kalen doubled over in laughter. Laughing harder when noticing my flat expression. If not mate bonded, I would have relished this bit of news. And Kalen knew it.

Taryn growled, an adorably impatient sound, and I pet her face. "Calm, my swearing sweet potato."

The furious look she delivered nearly had me doubling over with Kalen. "You swore on the stolen baked potato, *Finny*, not me."

"You bargained on a potato?" Kalen asked, falling into another fit of laughter.

"That he did," Taryn confirmed, a smug smile pulling on her lips. "Now one of you explain before I punch you both in your pointy-eared Corbie faces."

"Oisín means 'small deer,' in our language," I began. "And 'fianna' is another fae word for 'deer.'"

"Fianna as in the war band Finn MacCool led?" she asked.

I could see the wheels spinning in her eyes. The Maiden's riddle was clever, even for the likes of me. If not for Kalen, I probably wouldn't have connected the clues.

"The same word, aye. Long story, involving a woman a druid had turned into a deer, whom Finn married, turning her back into a woman, and . . . well, do you know Lady Fianna Winslow?"

Her face pulled into a grimace of disgust. "The woman who collects young elven males to 'work' in her home?" She did air quotes with "work."

Kalen grinned. "Finn, lad, I feel nothing but pity for your shite luck, I do."

Taryn snorted. "Good thing you're a fluffy bunny for the mature lasses, *Frank*."

"Try not to get jealous this time, Rynnie." My lips twitched.

"I wasn't jealous."

"You had murder eyes."

Taryn pointed at her face. "I always have murder eyes when I look at you, Finn Brannon."

"Oh love . . ." A sensual smile flirted across my lips. "The way you seduce me with your pining looks."

"Stars," she groaned under her breath. "Do you never stop?"

Slowly, I ran a finger down my chest, down my stomach because no, I didn't ever stop. And, to my delight, her gaze traveled the path I made for her, lower, lower. "Ask nicely and I'll let you feast your hungry eyes on my energetic flesh one more time," I said in a huskier voice than I intended.

The mood instantly shifted between us.

A slight crackle of rising heat.

My mind spun back to the inn, to the feel of her bare skin pressed to mine, the way she perfectly fit curled up against me. From the flush of her cheeks, her mind had traveled back there too.

"Is this your dramatic way of asking for me to check on your wound, Finny?" The words were a challenge, but the delivery was breathy.

Fiery suns in the sky help me . . .

Steal a thousand kisses from my lips, Finnan.

Blood rushed to my groin and I swallowed thickly. I would swear on all the ancient amulets in the entire Kingdom of Carran for just one night to make her mine. When our mate bond dissolved, I wanted all other males compared to me and found lacking. I wanted to be the only magic she craved. Let it drive her to insanity like she was driving me by not recalling a single moon blasted word of her confession.

Kalen peered between us, then shot me a were-you-kicked-in-the-head scrunch of the face. I casually touched the ravens on my wrist and Kalen nodded. He understood.

This building fire between me and Taryn could only be that, I reminded myself. A binding of convenience. One I will have paid for with years stolen from my life.

The reminder sobered me and I stepped away from Taryn.

We needed to see guild master and get this over with.

"See you later at Prim, mate," I said to Kal.

"Be brave," he whispered. "Niall is in a chipper mood today." And with that warning, he sauntered off into the clouds of billowing steam through the alley back toward Crescent Street.

Taryn and I eyed each other for a long second, then I gestured with my head for her to follow.

"Kalen a Caravan fae too?" she asked me a minute later.

"Not the same Traveler tribe as me, but aye. He was sold to Corbie when fourteen."

Her body stiffened. "Do Caravan fae often sell their children?"

"Only the Outsider ones."

We fell silent after that. It was a harsh truth of being born in The Wilds. We were a dying race of fae. Perhaps our numbers were stronger in other kingdoms. Actually, I knew they were. But in Carran, we held little value to the mortals beyond our resource rich forests and rivers.

Caravan fae were the only mainlanders who took in my kind and only because the kingdom gave them a one-time payment for our care. Despite making us second class citizens and, in many cases, slaves, most Travelers were decent Fair Folk, and family centered, too. I missed the gatherings and games and story nights. But they didn't marry Outsiders, what they called anyone who wasn't a Traveler true blood. And when a tribe found themselves in trouble with the law, which was often given their night markets, it was the male Outsiders close to fifteen, a Caravan's marrying age, they offered up in payment. A trade for continued freedom and to protect their unwed daughters from polluting the Traveler lines.

There was a hefty number of orphaned wild fae to trade, too.

It didn't take long to reach the gate into Primry Green. Taryn peered around, returning the threatening stares directed her way by other Corbies. Niall was shouting at a Corbie when Taryn and I entered the warehouse and rounded toward his office.

"Lovely gent," Taryn muttered under breath. "A right fatherly type."

A quip died on my tongue. My heart dropped to my churning stomach. Why did this feel more like marching to a death sentence?

"Off with ye," guild master shouted.

My Corbie brother dragged by me, his fists curled.

I drew in a shaking breath. Taryn was a white sheet beside me. But she lifted her chin and squared her shoulders as we stepped into guild master's office.

"Ye failed, Corbie." Niall fixed his fury onto Taryn. "And ye

111

stole property from Black Beak."

Shite. He already knew. Of course, he did. Damn spy ravens.

"We didn't have a choice—"

"Davis!" Niall snapped and a large man stepped from the shadows. "Show our latest Corbie guest around. Shut the door behind you. Gan, hold Finn."

The behemoth of a man grabbed Taryn and yanked her through the door. I charged after them, growling, but Gan stepped in front of my path.

"We can't be separated more than fif—"

The magic flung me toward Taryn. A magic so strong, I took Gan with me.

I braced for impact right as we crashed into the closed door and kept sailing at high speed. Splintered wood flew around us. I just had time to cover my head with my arms when Gan and Davis collided in a grunting heap of muscle. Taryn, who was gripped in Davis's hands, dropped to the stone floor and, before she could protect herself, hit her head.

Fury ripped through me. I snarled. Like a beast. Baring my teeth at Gan and Davis in a growl of warning, I crawled over to my mate and pulled her to my chest.

"Taryn, love," I whispered, my pulse pounding violently in my ears. If she so much as had a scratch, I would rip the bulky arms off Davis's body. My fingers swept over her head, her face.

"I'm fine," she ground out—and froze when noting the feral gleam in my eyes.

Aye, these are murder eyes, Rynnie.

"B3H9 reported true," Niall said.

"You endangered her life on purpose?" My growl halted Niall's approach. Finally realizing my mate bond was turning me into a territorial, protective animal, he backed up a step. *Now run so I can hunt you down.*

"Ye're under a curse that harms Corbie, Finnan Ó Brannon. Failed yer job and stole from Corvus. Aye, I needed proof before dealing with Black Beak." He paused a beat, then added, "And before dealing with ye."

Niall pulled out a cigarette and a match, struck it on the brick wall and lit up. Sucking in a draw, he slowly blew out, his eyes trained on me as I continued to cradle Taryn, my chest heaving, my canines still bared. "Ye know yer debt—"

"I know the fae laws, mortal," I seethed in return. "You can demand nothing from me for another twelve days. But please do. I want to dance on your grave of eternal bad luck."

Niall flicked his ashes and sneered down at us. "If yer arse isn't in my chair at the crack of dawn on the thirteenth day, ye'll be marked. No mercy. Understand, Corbie?"

I didn't answer him. Instead, I gently helped Taryn to her feet, guided her around Davis and Gan, and led her into the junk-yard.

Once outside, I closed my eyes and lifted my face to the sky to gather my wits. The afternoon sun warmed my flushing skin while a breeze cooled the rage. I was shaking. My breath, my body. My muscles were begging for a fight.

"Finn . . ." Taryn whispered and I slowly looked her way. "Corbie doesn't deserve our mainland catch. Let's trade for new clothes and proper baths."

A smile softened my lips. "You just want another glimpse of my energetic flesh."

I joked, but the smile was forced.

"Maybe I do."

Our eyes locked.

Feck. Me.

I was officially shoved from my mood and into an entirely different heated one.

"How else can I change the dressing on your wound, Finny?" she added with a wink and sauntered off.

And stars above, I followed her like a dog on a leash.

Chapter Twelve

TARYN HUNT

What's taking so long?"

Finn's hurried whisper jolted another spike of adrenaline into my pumping veins. Tying a front lacing corset was easy. Buttoning up the gown's bodice proved a challenge, even for my thieving fingers.

"I can't button up—" My skin jumped at the sudden feel of fingers on my upper back. "A little warning next time."

He deftly began fastening my bodice and I tried not to blush. I was still flushed with racing nerves from using the servant passages to sneak into the guest rooms at the Palace of Stars. I had stolen many things these past few years, but not a silk gown. Lady Winslow, however, was attending the ball this night. A ball already underway below.

"Done."

I turned, cringing at the loud swishing sound of my skirts, to face him.

And, friends, my soul left my body. He was . . . falling stars . . . Finn in street clothes was dangerous enough. But in a fine tailcoat and dress shirt? My breath was coming quick. I blinked a few times to shake myself from these foreign feelings. I was already muddled by his fierce, animalist reaction to the Corbie guild master two days prior. It was terrifying and liquified my beating heart into moonlight.

Finn played with a wavy tendril of my earthen hair, seeming equally as awestruck as me. Looking away, I pulled on gloves to cover my ravens, then smoothed out invisible wrinkles on my dark teal blue gown and cleared my throat. I hadn't worn a dress in three or four years now, preferring boy's breeches.

"I don't know how to fashion my hair—"

"You're beautiful," he whispered.

I shrugged. "A fine gown and jewels would pretty up a pig."

"Taryn," he said softly, "Your beauty was legendary when covered in bog mud."

Pale green eyes roamed down my silk-draped body before slowly drifting upward to meet mine. Another blush crept up my neck. The slight part of his lips and broody scowl between his brows, the way light and shadows caressed the planes of his face threatened to steal all the breath from my corset-squeezed lungs.

No one looked at me the way he did. No one had ever cared for me the way he did too.

"Let's go," I said, all business. If I didn't, I would become a sighing puddle of silk on the floor. And I refused to be like all the other girls in his presence, no matter how much I thought about his lips on mine, his fingers possessively sliding across my skin.

We had a curse to break.

Finn followed me from behind the changing screen. We crept through the room and out into the empty hallway. My pulse was pounding in my ears. Finn and I were too rough around the edges for fine society. I didn't have the slightest idea of how to communicate using a fan let alone female etiquette in gatherings. At least I was being presented as a married woman if we were forced to socialize. I mean, I *was* a married woman.

I bit back a growl.

With arms looped together, we descended the grand stairs to the main foyer. Music drifted over the marble floors and echoed off the alabaster ceilings.

I began to gape and remembered my fake manners.

There were so many attendees, my eyes didn't know where to settle. Finn ushered us into the ballroom and I had to keep my jaw from hitting the floor. Candlelight reflected off a midnight sky ceiling dotted with glass constellations. The twinkling effect was pure magic and created golden falling stars over the dancers.

A corner of Finn's mouth hooked up, a mischievous glint in his eyes, right before he pulled me onto the floor. I tried not to squeal as he swept me into the music. They were playing a familiar reel, a faerie tune I had always enjoyed.

Weaving his fingers with mine, we spun beside the other dancers.

A disorienting, dizzy rush buzzed down my limbs.

We had bargained with a fae witch, fought a bog monster together, bathed in a moonlit mineral spring, braved the rain and traded work for a room at an inn. And now we pretended to be high society while dancing to a commoner's song. Would a life with Finn at my side always be this adventurous?

We stepped a lively beat in a line and I almost closed my eyes to revel in the melody. A second later, the song returned to a slower rhythm and, yet, my pulse quickened. Finn wrapped an arm around my waist, our hands connecting above our heads as we turned in place. I laughed. At the sound, Finn bit down on a waggish grin. My head was spinning faster than the choreography. Faster than the quick thumping of the song's bodhrán drum. Falling stars lit our shared smiles as we danced. And . . . I felt myself falling too. Moon above, I hadn't felt this happy in an age.

Holding hands, we stepped toward the center floor and formed a circle with the other dancers, our fingers untwining to meet in the middle to form a star, then we all moved clockwise. Four beats later, we switched direction, putting out our opposite hand and moved counterclockwise.

The reel ended a couple measures later and I fell into breathless laughter against Finn. He pulled me in close until my cheek pressed to his chest and his arms circled my waist. I couldn't remember the last time I had enjoyed myself or felt so free.

"I would bargain on a hundred potatoes to dance with you all night, Rynnie love," he whispered into my hair. "But our target is close by."

Rynnie love.

I wasn't sure why that made my heart skip faster than dancing a reel.

"Where?"

He didn't need to answer.

A woman with unnaturally radiant skin, beautifully curled blonde hair—wearing a low-cut emerald green gown, a large ruby necklace resting on her cleavage—tracked Finn as he escorted me off the floor. Several females trailed his movements, too, and I had to resist the urge to glare at each one of them. Instead, I casually peered up at Finn. A seductive tilt played his lips, his eyes predatory as he made an open show of enjoying Lady Winslow's curves. This was the plan. I knew this but seeing it in action twisted a flame of fury in my gut . . . which confused me.

He wasn't mine. I had no claim on him.

Finn leaned down to whisper in my ear, his heated gaze locked onto Lady Winslow's the entire time. "I only want you, Taryn Hunt." He bowed, kissing my hand and, while lowered, his gaze slammed into mine. "*Only* you, love."

My pulse caught fire. I couldn't breathe.

What did he mean he wanted *only* me? Was this him speaking or our mate bond? And why did it feel like "love" wasn't said as typical alley boy street slang but as an actual endearment?

Finn strode away. And stars, I was a mess. He had the knack of easily turning my world upside down.

Blowing out a slow breath, I gathered my unraveling thoughts and followed not too far behind while pretending to look for someone. My gaze jumped around and . . . landed on a familiar pair of hazel eyes in palace livery. Tommy? The Black Beak's gaze flicked to Finn then back to me. *Shite.* Was the Amulet of Oisín his assigned catch? Or something else? I turned, as if not recognizing him, and glanced in Finn's direction.

The arrogant elf casually leaned a shoulder on the wall. His head dipped toward Lady Winslow's, pale green eyes holding hers beneath fallen strands of dark green hair. He trailed a finger down her arm as they spoke and I grit my teeth.

I only want you, Taryn Hunt.

Confusion crept back into focus. Was this all to ensure I didn't make a scene and ruin our plan? Watching Finn, I was suddenly aware of just how sensually he moved. He oozed every fantasy females desired and could steal a heart with a well-planned smile and silver-tongued confession.

Like in the pond. Like at the inn. Like just now before approaching our target.

"Your dance partner appears heartbroken," a cultured mainlander voice said in an intentionally loud voice. Finn arched a brow at me and I blinked out of the trance I was apparently in to find Lady Winslow chuckling at me.

"She likes to seduce me," Finn replied, a humored twist to his lips, though his eyes were soft and strangely protective when meeting my gaze. I almost rolled mine in reply. He turned back to Lady Winslow and, in a low, husky voice, said, "But she doesn't have what I want."

"And what do you want?" Her fingers played with a button on his shirt.

I partially turned away, pretending not to notice Tommy's hot stare while also pretending to be interested in finding a new dance partner. But I continued to watch from the corner of my eye.

"I know your tastes, Lady Winslow," Finn said with a devilish smile. That smile. *That stars damned smile.* "Let's not play games, aye?"

Her finger traced down his chest. "What if I like games?"

"Dangerous..." His gaze traveled to her mouth. "To tempt an elf with games." She laughed, a low seductive sound that clawed down my spine. Finn's smirk widened and he leaned in closer. "Let's go somewhere private."

Not giving her a chance to reply, Finn took her arm in his and wheeled her toward the balcony, as planned. I followed after them, sliding a fan from a girl's wrist as I passed. The moment he and Lady Winslow passed through the opening and into night, he walked her into the velvet drapes out of sight—and kissed her.

Dragon fire burned just beneath my skin. His kiss was fake. But what if it wasn't? What if Finn actually desired to kiss her?

I only want you, Taryn Hunt.

Dark skies, how I ached for that to be true. To be genuinely wanted—by him.

I snapped the fan open, not needing to act as if I were flushed as I stood by the balcony opening. Lady Winslow began unbuttoning his coat, the top of his shirt. Finn turned her, so her back faced the opening, then tangled his fingers into her hair, a thumb caressing the skin just above the amulet's clasp—my cue.

Quickly, I tucked the fan into my bodice and tiptoed onto the balcony, grateful the music inside and street sounds outside hid the swish of my gown's skirts. Finn's eyes locked onto mine as he left her mouth to trail kisses down her jaw, down her neck. A wide-eyed expression that shouted to "hurry up." I bared my teeth at him but went to work.

The moment my fingers touched the amulet's clasp, Finn returned to her mouth. Her hand trailed down his bare chest. It took everything in me not to choke her with the chain I was unfastening. That damn elf found my furious gaze again, his eyes appearing to laugh at my reaction. He found this funny? His fingers splayed down her jaw and neck while cradling her face. That moment, I unhooked the clasp and it fell into Finn's waiting hands.

I tiptoed back into the ballroom and fanned myself once more to appear natural to anyone who passed by.

A shriek echoed from behind.

"The feck!"

"Return the amulet to me, boy, or suffer a curse."

I peered in and my heart stopped. The beautiful woman who was once Lady Winslow had withered into a hunched over, age spotted, wrinkled old hag with patchy white hair and sharp yellow teeth. Finn started gagging and I burst into laughter. *Yeah, Finny, you passionately kissed that.*

The hag screamed words I couldn't make out and Finn bolted, grabbing my arm.

I laughed while we ran from the palace.

I laughed as we dashed into the alleys toward Beggar's Hole, where we had stashed our change of clothing and meager belongings. Stars, I hadn't laughed this much in years. Finn was laughing too. What a horrifying, unexpected twist. An amulet from the Land of Youth . . . *Gods.*

We climbed up the abandoned warehouse stairs, a building located a couple of blocks from the Palace of Stars. On our floor, we barely made it into the room we had staked for ourselves when Finn grabbed me by the waist and swung me around to face him.

Our eyes locked. Our breaths came fast. His gaze lingered on my lips a few wild heartbeats before he pushed me against the brick wall and kissed my laughter.

Chapter Thirteen

TARYN HUNT

What are you doing?" I asked in-between kisses. "Stealing my third of a thousand kisses from you," he whispered back.

His mouth crashed onto mine in the next breath. And moon above . . . he consumed me. I lost all thought, all reason. Only feeling flooded my senses until I thought I would drown in them. Feelings for him, us. What could be. What I yearned to have but never would.

My hands pressed to the bare skin of his chest. I really should push him away.

There was no turning back if we crossed this line. And . . . I didn't think my heart would survive losing him afterward.

Still, I continued to unbutton his dress shirt, making his breath flutter. Without breaking our kiss, he tossed the suit jacket, waistcoat, and dress shirt to the floor. His forearms caged me in close to his body and our kiss caught fire. The skin beneath my fingers was smooth and warm. All hard lines and toned muscle.

This was a dream.

It had to be.

What I felt right now was otherworldly.

Breaking our kiss, he spun me around and gently pressed me to the wall. I gasped at the cold feel of the brick against my cheek. What was he doing . . . *Oh. Stars.* He dragged a canine down my neck and, friends, my knees buckled. I was genuinely swooning and I didn't care if he knew. Finn trailed kisses along my throat, his mouth dipping lower as his fingers quickly worked the buttons of my bodice. The fabric fell away. I pulled the sleeves down my arms and threw the garment beside his.

The heat of his body leaned into me. "Come, love," he whispered in my ear.

Before I could reply, Finn scooped me into his arms and strode over to our makeshift cot. Gently he laid me atop our thin blanket and straddled my hips. Dark teal blue silk pooled around where we lay from my skirt. Moonlight caressed the sculpted lines of his chest and stomach, the curves of his arms and broad shoulders. The quickened breath from my lungs strained against my corset.

"There is no beauty that compares to yours, Taryn Hunt."

Finn's fingers traced the shape of me—the soft swell of my corseted breasts, the curves of my waist, my hips. My eyes fluttered closed on a soft moan. I didn't know a touch could be so poetic. Or confess a thousand longings in just one caress. But I did know this: those fingers claimed ownership with each brush. And like a fool, I let him. He could possess me entirely right now and I wouldn't stop him. Even though I should.

I really, really should.

This was a terrible idea.

Life was complicated enough without breaking rule three—especially with him.

Finn lowered his mouth to mine and softly blinked. "In a different life, I think I could fall hard for you."

My pulse stuttered a beat. He wanted to fall for . . . *me*?

I only want you, Taryn Hunt.

My own parents didn't want me. But my rival? Why? Did he tell all the girls this? Not that it mattered, whether the words were true or a trick. There could be no future where we remained bound as mates. There could be no future with *anyone* if we wanted to earn our freedom.

Right now, though? We could indulge in a Seren fantasy. I desperately longed for one of my own with him too—where he truly wanted me and I could allow my heart to fall for his. Where my mortal life was as long as his so we could grow old together. *Close your eyes, rule three.*

I cupped Finn's face. "Let's relocate to somewhere homier."

He leaned his forehead onto mine. "To a place with a misty mountain view."

"With a patch of lawn for a garden and plenty of room for a bairn or two to romp around."

"And my wife, in the kitchen . . ." he whispered, his voice catching. "My wife . . ." he couldn't finish his sentence, too overcome.

This false freedom would end.

A strange thought when we couldn't escape one another. Yet,

here we were, desiring to be even closer. As if the thought of separation would shatter newfound pieces of ourselves.

Perhaps we could still steal tiny slices of forever once curse free.

And I knew how.

I slid my fingers up to his messy knot of hair and pulled on the tie. "Steal another kiss and don't stop." Dark green strands fell to his shoulders and tickled my cheek. "Even after our curse is broken, keep stealing kisses from my lips."

"Is this a bargain?" he asked me.

"Yes, promise me, Finnan."

In the distance, Seren's clock rang the midnight bells right as his lips fell to my neck. In all our finery, I could almost imagine this was our wedding day. Finn kissed the hollow of my throat, kissed my collarbone, his mouth branding my skin wherever he touched me. Moving back up my neck, Finn licked my earlobe with the tip of his tongue, then whispered, "I promise you."

A heady sweetness charged the air around us. My body buzzed with electricity at the delicious feel of his pressed to mine, of his hand cradling my cheek, the other playing with the laces of my stolen corset.

Finn dragged his nose along my jaw, whispering my name.

I knew what he was asking me. And I sank my fingers into his hair, breathing "yes." A plea, a prayer. Permission.

His mouth crushed mine.

And I wasn't sure if I existed anymore.

Or wanted to.

The searing lick of fire in each stroke of his tongue unraveled me until I was only gasping breath and pooling sensation. I became the night sky, every twinkling star above, the moon, the sun, and every wish made upon the heavens.

Entwining his fingers with mine, Finn pinned our joined hands beside my face. His other hand pulled on my corset laces and a shiver of pleasure pebbled across my skin. A little voice in the back of my head warned that I was just another dalliance. That I was lonely and never realized how much so until I tasted what could be. And yet, I didn't want this cosmic rush of spinning out of control with him to end.

I died to the melodic slow dance of his lips across mine and resurrected to the possessive rhythm he directed at every rapid beat of my thundering heart. His touch was gentle, each tug on my laces slow. A building my body blissfully surrendered to—

"Taryn Hunt!"

A sharp tap on the window behind us echoed in the warehouse. I startled a yelp. Finn's head snapped up. His body moved to protectively cover me.

Another sharp rap. "Taryn Hunt!"

Finn's body sagged. "A bloody raven."

I closed my eyes in a long, anxious blink. Blowing out a slow breath, I pushed Finn back and awkwardly rolled to my knees. How did females function in all this fabric? The amount of silk puddled around me was ridiculous. A cold breeze chilled my flushing skin and I looked down. *Stars!* The brocade corset wrapped around my torso was halfway unraveled. I covered myself with an arm, pretending that mortification wasn't quickly painting my skin scarlet. Finn picked up our thin blanket and, while looking away, pulled it over my shoulders as a shawl.

"Taryn Hunt!" The damn raven repeated with three beaked taps on the glass.

I opened the window and the bird flew in, landing on a nearby shelf. "Taryn Hunt, Black Beak has summoned you, but—"

"Why?" I asked the raven. "They can't demand anything from me for another ten days and they know this."

The raven hopped down the shelf closer to me. "You need to run, Taryn Hunt."

My eyes narrowed. "Are you S725?"

"The amulet." The raven cocked her head to look at me with one single black eye. "A Black Beak job."

My heart dropped into my stomach. Tommy was assigned to steal the amulet; I knew it. And now Finn had stolen from Black Beak twice. Turning in the amulet wasn't an option. But spy ravens would always find us, so running was useless.

I absently rubbed at the tattoos on my wrist and stilled. Why was my Black Beak guild mark fading? The mate bond one with Finn was solid and dark. But my Thieves' Guild mark was slowly disappearing before my eyes.

"Finn?" I squeaked, pointing at my wrist.

He paled but didn't look surprised. What was going on? He still had two solid marks.

"Run and hide," the raven cawed and flapped her wings. "Black Beak will hunt you."

"Why are you helping us?"

"The Maiden sends her greetings."

My brows shot up. The Sisters Three were aiding us?

"Wait!" I shouted as the raven alighted into the air. "Do you know where the tower of Corvus Rook is?"

"Stellar Winds Casi—" The raven's voice became an undecipherable caw as she sailed through the open window.

Oh gods . . .

My teeth set on edge as I lifted my wrist and stared at the smooth skin where a bonded raven once soared.

Why did it have to be *that* casino of all places?

Shite!

No, I had a bigger question first.

I shut the window and quickly spun on my heel toward Finn. We stared at each other for several long seconds. The moonlight caressed the hard lines and curves of his body and I . . . I felt exposed. Had he used coercion magic to manipulate me into trusting him? Into giving my body to him? The violation returned in a sickening wave and I was fifteen again. A different male elf, but it was all the same. All they did was take advantage of mortal girls who didn't have magic to resist theirs.

He stepped toward me. "Taryn—"

"Do not riddle me," I snapped. "Don't trick me into seeing a reality you paint for me either."

The softness in his eyes hardened. "I am *nothing* like *him*."

"I'm to believe you?" I balled my hand into a fist. "How many times have you used coercion magic on me?"

A muscle ticked along his jaw. "Twice—"

"TWICE?!"

"Only to protect you!" he shouted back.

"So you say. But I will never know, will I?" I pointed to my wrist. "What happened to my Thieves' Guild mark? Why do you still have one?"

Finn nervously licked his lips. "I own you, remember?"

"You said I was now a Corbie."

"No," he said slowly. "I said you would live with me at Prim."

I growled in frustration. "Speak plainly, Finnan!"

"You're debt free, Taryn. Six days have passed since we bonded as mates. My bride price to Black Beak was Corbie paying off your debt, a transaction that is now complete," he gritted out, baring his teeth.

"Free . . ." I whispered under my breath, unable to comprehend the meaning.

Angry tears reddened Finn's eyes. "Aye, and when we break this curse, you'll be free of me too."

Was this the heartbreak I tasted on his lips at the pond? The heartbreak in his eyes at the inn before we left and again on the ferry?

"For five days," I choked out, "you knew the price of our marriage and didn't give me the option to break our binds."

"Because it was *my* mistake, not yours—"

You were a mistake, my father's slurring voice echoed in my head.

"—and I can protect you best against the guilds as your bonded mate."

I vowed to put you above all others, that includes my own needs.

Nausea painfully churned in my gut.

All of his care and protection? It was *only* his binding vows. There was no real affection for me.

You were a mistake . . .

Stars, I was going to vomit.

"Leave Seren and don't look back, lass." Every word Finn spoke was tight. "Open an apothecary shop like you promised me. Fall in love, have bairns. Dozens of them."

The breath seized in my lungs. "Finn—"

"No pity!" he shouted. "No fussing!"

Our eyes locked. But I couldn't look at him, not for long, and grabbed my spare clothing. Brushing by him, I marched behind a tall shelf to change.

Mistake or not, I didn't ask him to take on my debt or indenture himself longer to break our fifteen feet of freedom curse.

Freedom.

Fury thrummed in my veins. It was a living, writhing beast. I wanted to scream, to throw rusted machine parts in this factory out the windows just to hear the glass shatter—like me.

He kissed me.

Kissed me knowing I could leave Seren and never look back. Knowing I lived with the grief of believing myself years away from paying off my newly incurred debts. That I would *never* be able to free him in return.

Gods, he *owned* me. He *bought* me.

And knowing this, knowing I did not, he kissed me and asked permission to do more.

But it was just his fecking vows kissing me—not him.

A dark, breathy laugh left me.

The first male who kissed me with promises of marriage broke my heart when he left me to pay for his coerced crimes.

But this male . . . the one I was married to in convenience? He broke my heart by paying for all of mine then kissing me as if it were an act of devotion instead of a mistake. As if, given the choice, he would sacrifice himself for my debts, for my protection and care, all over again.

I couldn't bear it.

Guilt was stealing my breath. My lungs were burning. My head nauseatingly dizzy.

Seven years I had shared Seren's streets with Finnan Ó Brannon and not one nice word between us. I have watched him with other girls, taking his pleasure to satisfy their fantasies, then walking away without even a parting glance.

He kissed me, deeply. Passionately.

And I let him, fooling myself that this was all real.

Bile burned my throat. I pressed a hand to my middle to ease the nausea.

Out of all the debts I have owed and could never repay, this one hurt the most.

Chapter Fourteen

FINN BRANNON

I studied the wound on my side. It hadn't troubled me in a couple of days. But a new tenderness plagued me. My skin was hot to the touch and turning a purplish color around the laceration where the scab had re-opened.

Glancing over my shoulder, I double-checked that Taryn was still asleep. Satisfied, I lifted my shirt higher to check on the large bruise on my left pectoral. The color was now a mottled yellow. But that clawed wound . . . my brows pushed together.

The hag who had glamoured herself as Lady Winslow must have cursed me like she had threatened. It was the only thing that made sense.

I battled if I should tell Taryn.

No, the lass was strung tighter than a lyre string since the raven interrupted us the night before last. She didn't make a pretty sound when plucked either.

A bite of sadness pinched my gut and gnawed endlessly in

my chest. I had kissed a lot of girls. But Taryn's lips were made for mine. And I was obsessed. Time stood still those few beautiful moments. I couldn't drink her in fast enough. The taste of her skin, the softness of her mouth, the sound of pleasure on her breath.

Make my heart your next catch.

Dropping the hem of my shirt, I sighed and resigned myself to another day of losing my mind and Taryn's snappy ire. She didn't trust me and I didn't trust her. This was true before we were forced to endure each other's company. But now our hearts were involved. No matter how many walls she threw in my face, I heard her desire when Seren's coercion magic stripped her bare. I knew the truth—truth she didn't see. Or didn't want to see.

And it messed with me. Without question, I was falling for Taryn Hunt. Falling fast and falling hard. Would I feel as intensely once our bond ended, though?

My gaze caressed the sweep of her cheeks, the flush of her lips.

She regretted kissing me. The look of horror on her face still echoed in my mind's eye. If she thought me only capable of cheap, meaningless fun, why did she kiss me back? And make me promise to kiss her after our mate bond was no more? We had a bargain now. Did she manipulate me? And for what reason? The sickened pallor of her skin when learning of her bride price gutted me. It was the look of a girl who feared the male before her expected her body in payment for his grand gesture. Worse, that he had tricked her specifically to own her body. I could be an arsehole, but suns above, I wasn't depraved.

She owed me nothing.

I didn't want anyone to ever owe me a damn thing.

I understood why she didn't trust me, though. By the stars, I would get that male's name and repay the kindness a hundred-fold. But now I had a new reason not to trust her.

She knew she was free. And she believed I expected favors for it.

Survival was the louder voice for us indentured thieves. Louder than friendship, louder than romance. We were so starved for self-ownership, morals didn't exist when freedom could.

And why I never told her.

Of course, her raven mark with Black Beak would disappear. I was an eejit.

Eight more days.

The ground was cold where I plopped down beside my mate who wasn't my mate but may also be my soulmate. *Thanks for the irritating riddle, Crone.* Despite our spotty sleep, we needed to hash out a casino heist plan and move to keep Black Beak on their toes. The tension was too unbearable yesterday to have any form of reasonable discussion.

I drew in a tight breath. *Be brave, lad.*

"Rise and shine, my Pegasus glitter beam of sunshine." I nudged her shoulder then quickly retracted my hand.

Taryn groaned into her arm and peeked open her eyes a sliver. Seeing me, she shut her eyes and rolled over. "Figures," she mumbled.

"That I am more handsome in reality than in dreams?" I asked innocently, hoping she'd playfully push back. *Please, lass. Take the bait.*

She huffed a disgusted sound, then buried her face into her arms and mumbled, "Morning people are the actual worst."

Well, that was an improvement from yesterday. I would take anything at this point.

As silently as possible, I scooted closer to her, lowered my mouth to her ear and, not-so-quietly, said, "Morning breath greetings that reek of fermented fish are the actual worst." She jumped with a squeak. I leaned back and continued, "Don't ask me how I know." I pretended to shudder.

Taryn's entire face twisted into sleepy fury. It was so adorable, I burst into loud laughter. Rising stars, I could happily wake to that every morning. Alas, my wee feisty potato didn't feel the same. Baring her teeth was the only warning I received before she launched herself at me.

Her shoulder slammed into my chest and knocked the air my from lungs. The next second, I was falling. We hit the stone floor with a grunt. Pain shot from my wound and I winced. Did that stop me from laughing, though?

"Call me a beam of sunshine one more time!" She threw a punch toward my chest and I caught her hand. "I dare you!"

A smirk teased a corner of my mouth. I lifted my head toward hers and taunted, "Need to work on that left hook . . . *sunshine.*" I ended with a wink, then quickly rolled out from beneath her.

Taryn heaved a sigh that was more like a groan with a side dish of a guttural scream tossed in.

"I didn't say 'beam.'" I lifted my shoulder in a humored shrug. She opened her mouth to curse my riddling ways, but I placed a finger to her pretty lips with a "Shhh . . ." before she could.

Gritting her teeth, she smacked my hand away. "Finnan—"

"Save the fire, Rynnie. We need to move."

The blood visibly drained from her face and her eyes snapped to the door. "Black Beak found us?"

"No," I quickly answered her. "But if Corbie learns that we have the Amulet of Oisín, we'll have two guilds on the hunt."

"Corbie probably already knows."

"Aye," I agreed. "Our rival guild bosses are as thick as thieves, it seems."

"Shite." Those large doe eyes found mine then quickly looked away. A heaviness lined her weary gaze. Clearing her throat, she asked, "As in Corvus and Rook might be brothers? Or mates?"

I nodded my head. "Or the same male. Maybe female."

"You believe they're fae too?"

"There's no question on that, love."

"Don't call me *love*." Her request was quiet but sharp, the words an arrow to my chest. Taryn sucked in her bottom lip and peered toward the dusty window. "We'll need to enter Stellar Winds Casino from the roof."

I leaned onto my hands to stretch my back. Fire spread across my middle and I flinched. A sharp breath strangled in my throat; I clamped down on my jaw. Taryn, thankfully, had turned her attention from the window to plucking loose threads from our thin blanket and didn't see me.

"We enter from the roof and then what?" I asked, hoping my voice sounded normal.

"There's an attic. It's where he and—"

Holy mother of stars . . . *This* was the casino she robbed?

"His name," I growled.

Taryn laughed, but it was full of venom.

"Is he still on the island?"

Her gaze *finally* leveled onto mine. "From the attic, we can slip into the walls and travel between rooms unseen."

"Bootlegger walls?" I asked, my mouth falling open.

"Throughout the whole casino."

A moan left me. That was so sexy. The danger was almost worth it simply for the experience of moving through the walls like the street rats we were.

Taryn wrinkled her nose.

Biting back a quip, I reached for my bag. "Tonight, then?" My fingers rummaged around until I found the beef jerky we traded a pickpocketed necklace for. I grabbed a slice for me and tossed the remaining pieces to Taryn in a bundled cloth. I had made sure she had continual food since our night at the inn. I would thieve all day and night for her to have three meals a day. Even if meager ones, like right now.

She bit into the jerky and chewed, her eyes jumping from object to object in the large room we slept in, a warehouse in Corbie territory. "Do you know what the Eye of Lugh looks like?"

"No, but I could guess."

Her gaze drifted to mine and she gestured with the dried meat to continue.

"Lugh is our sun god, a powerful warrior," I said, tearing into a piece of jerky. While chewing, I added, "He has two ravens that attend to all his needs."

141

"Two ravens . . ." she repeated. Our eyes locked.

I snorted. The Maiden was a clever one, she was. Kalen would appreciate this riddle.

"Is this eye an actual eye?" Her face grimaced. "Tell me we're not thieving the eye of an actual god?"

"It is an actual eye, Rynnie." I kept my voice gravely serious, though I wasn't.

She peered at the jerky and lowered it to her lap. "This is the part where you say but not *not* an eye, right?"

"The Eye of Lugh is an eye," I continued just as serious before, "but not all eyes need a body to see."

Taryn's face fell. "You're so full of shite."

My lips twitched. "Do you know what the Caravan fae call an 'eye?'"

"If you don't get to the point in the next breath I will—"

"A crystal ball, love," I finished, then bit into the jerky. "An all-*seeing* orb."

I stilled, realizing I called her "love." But she didn't seem to notice.

Taryn's brows scrunched together. "Eye of Lugh," she murmured in thought. "So this all-seeing orb has the power of a god to control Black Beak and Corbie? The two ravens are us but also the guilds, yeah?"

Oh.

Stars bless me.

I could kiss her. But our rebuilding trust was a fragile, wobbly thing.

"Look at you, riddling like a clever fae," I said instead.

She ignored me. "That would explain how the ravens are controlled and connected to us through all-*seeing* magic." Pointing her piece of jerky at me, the wheels spinning in her eyes, she asked, "Is Lugh code for the sun, then?"

"Of course." I pointed my piece of jerky back at her. "Probably why Black Beak and Corbie were dispatched to find the Crone's weather ring, aye?"

One, single dark brow arched. "Why does the Maiden want the Eye of Lugh? Does she plan to control us next?"

I cocked my head. It was a fair question. I wasn't sure why she wanted the Dobhar-chú tooth. The Amulet of Oisín was clearly to replace the Crone with the Maiden. I mildly gagged at the memory of kissing that hag. There were many fae tales of the Maiden using handsome young males to physically return her to power while in the Crone's body. Now I was a statistic.

"Finn."

I snapped from my traumatic thoughts. "The Maiden seems to already keep the company of ravens," I rushed out. "Does it matter what she uses the Eye for?"

Taryn tore into another piece of jerky while returning her gaze to the dusty windows and shrugged.

The only thing that mattered was that we break this curse and before our fifteen days were up.

We continued to eat in silence, both of us lost to our own thoughts. Afterward, Taryn bundled up the travel cot and blanket we bargained for with part of our mainlander catch.

While slipping between the shadows to a new building, and the two others later in the day, I tried not to care how she went out of her way to make as much space between our bodies as possible. Or how she turned her back to me when settled until we moved again.

Returning to Stellar Winds Casino couldn't be easy for her. I would destroy that male.

Chapter Fifteen

TARYN HUNT

For a few terrifying seconds, I flew across the air.

Finn's hand clamped tighter around mine. Thankfully it wasn't a far jump from this roof to the next. Though, when suspended thirty or so feet above the ground, in the dark of night, any amount of open air felt like a freefall grave.

We landed on wobbly legs. Promptly, I dropped Finn's hand and stepped away. He kept trying to chum things up between us, as if we never kissed each other like besotted, desperate fools. Or like he hadn't failed to disclose that he not only owned me, per fae laws, but he *bought* me. A bride price. Just thinking about it made me sick to my stomach.

One didn't thank the fae. Not unless they wanted to be beholden to them. I was already far too indebted to Finn.

Regardless of cultural differences, how could I possibly thank the one who had gambled and lost everything on me? A male who treated me with more care and protection than any other in this stars damned world? Not because he wanted to, though. That's the part that continually shattered me over and over and over again. No, his magic compelled him to place me above all others, as he vowed. There was no truth in it.

When our mate bond dissolved, he would resent me.

I was nothing more than a mistake, after all.

And I . . . I didn't know if my heart would survive it.

Yet, I couldn't stop yearning for what could never be with him.

Stars, it hurt to breathe. Grief pressed on my chest and I absently placed a hand to my heart to quiet the pain.

Finn glanced at me. "Only one more jump." His voice strained, far more than it should have been.

I narrowed my eyes. The gas lamps in the main corridors barely touched the roofs of the buildings along the main strip. Was his injury paining him? Noticing my inspection, he straightened and looked toward Stellar Winds Casino. Something was ailing him, his side or nerves or both.

I rubbed my temples.

We had moved three different times today. At each location, a raven found us and cawed our whereabouts—Corbie ravens linked to Finn's mark. I was now untraceable to Black Beak. A spy raven clearly told both guild masters the magical objects requested by the witch. Why else would the guilds be hounding us out? While troublesome, that wasn't what bothered me most: they clearly didn't care if we broke our curse. Which meant . . . they didn't care if we lived after the amulet was retrieved.

Fear pulsed right behind my eyes. A dull, throbbing ache. My clenched jaw didn't help.

I peered out over the roof. Only a handful of factories still in production possessed rusted ladders on their outer walls for boiler chimney repairs. Almost all buildings had roof access from inside. But, to get to Stellar Wind's rooftop, we had to leap from building to building. This next jump, however, stretched a wide alley.

Seven years ago, I used plank boards to walk across this gap. A resource Finn and I couldn't obtain in short order. Gaining access to the roof from inside the casino was impossible too.

So, our options were to either die jumping or die after a guild snatched the amulet from our possession. I swallowed against the thickening knot in my throat. This wouldn't be the first time Finn and I had faced death together.

A shudder wended down my spine.

Might as well get it over with.

I moved to angle past Finn. Cold fingers wrapped around my wrist and tugged me back. My gaze snapped first to his hand then to his pale eyes. But he wasn't looking at me. I turned and my stomach lurched. A black cloud of flapping wings was moving toward us.

Ravens.

A large conspiracy of ravens.

It was unmistakable despite the indigo night cloaked around us.

Dammit stars! The guilds knew where we were—again. It was at least two in the morning. Why were so many ravens still awake? And who reported us?

No words needed to be said. We had to reach the attic hatch

before the ravens reached us. I yanked Finn into motion, my hand clutched in his. We dashed toward the roofline that faced Stellar Winds. The alley between the nightclub we stood atop and the casino suddenly appeared too wide. Maybe it really was.

At the edge, Finn shouted, "Jump!"

We pushed off the roofline and . . . air. Night-kissed air drenched in steam from the smokestack beside us. My heart soared from my stomach to my tightening throat. Our trajectory was off, our leap not high enough. The alley was just slightly too wide. We weren't going to make it. Already I felt us sinking toward the cobbled street below.

The thunderous caws of ravens quaked down my bones. His fingers crushed mine. My hair whipped around my face. We were falling fast. I closed my eyes, not wanting to see the ground claim my death. A scream ripped from my lungs just as dozens of ravens pecked at my back, my arms, my legs, my hair—

Our bodies jolted in the air. A sudden stop that cut off my scream.

Finn started laughing, a breathy, disbelieving sound.

My eyes snapped open. What little blood was left in my head rushed to my trembling limbs. I couldn't believe what I was seeing. We were flying on the wings of ravens. They were carrying us to the Stellar Winds Casino roof. The nausea bubbling in my gut burned my throat. I was a few seconds from retching.

Finn squeezed my fingers and I chanced a look at him as we floated through the air. The look on his face stilled my barely pulsing heart—giddy adoration. As if he didn't know if he wanted to keep laughing for not splattering on the cobbled street below or kiss me to celebrate still being alive . . . as if raven talons hadn't dug into our bodies twenty or thirty feet above the ground. He was crazy. I could almost hear his voice behind that look too.

Oh, love, the way you seduce me with your falling-to-your-death ways.

Eejit—

A deafening chorus of caws pierced my ears. *Shite*, my ears could bleed, it was so loud.

I didn't have time to think about why the sudden ruckus. Within a single blink of my terror-stricken eyes, another conspiracy had arrived and began attacking our saviors. Wings beat faster all around us. The enemy ravens dove at the ones carrying us. We were so close to the roofline now. Just a couple more feet. Talons lost grip on my right leg. My body tilted and I cried out. My pulse violently pounded behind my ribs. The ravens still attached to my clothing beat faster, their caws echoing in my ringing ears. Just when I thought we wouldn't make it, both Finn and I sailed over the lip of the roofline.

A sob tightened in my chest.

The birds let go of my clothing to join the fray above our heads and in the alley. I landed onto the brick with a grunt. Black feathers littered the rooftop and floated around us. I scrambled to my feet and covered my ears to block out the piercing caws and screeching shouts. We needed to run. But Finn and I didn't get far. Ravens attacked my arms, pecked at my back, clawed at my head. I screamed and knocked them away with my hands.

Finn shouted my name, then grabbed me. I fought to break free, too wild with fear to understand it was him at first. Before

I could protest another second, he wrapped his arms around me protectively, covering my head with his hands. I wouldn't cry. I wouldn't vomit. I could hear the birds thump into his back and flap around his head. He held me tighter.

"We'll run on a count of three," he whispered in my ear.

"I can't breathe," I rasped out. My heart was pumping too fast. My hands shook violently.

"You can do this, lass," he reassured. "I'm right beside you, aye? How far are we from the hatch?"

"What if it doesn't open?"

"How far away is the hatch, Taryn?" he repeated.

"Straight line, halfway toward the opposite roof edge."

He nodded his head. "One . . . two . . . THREE!"

Grabbing Finn's hand, I charged across the bricked roof, my forearm in front of my face to block incoming birds. The moment we started moving, our allies surrounded us—daggering our attackers with their beaks or sinking talons into their flesh to haul the enemy ravens away from us.

Ten steps. Seven steps. Four, two . . .

I slid to a stop in front of the hatch and yanked on the door. It creaked open to my surprise. The room was pitch black. I didn't know what we were lowering into. If a rat or insect infestation would be our next nightmare. Finn grunted as another bird dove at him. *Shite, I need to get a grip.* Drawing in a tight breath, I crawled into the opening and lowered down the ladder on shaking legs. The hatch closed above me a couple of seconds later, sealing away what little light there was, but the sound of Finn descending the ladder comforted my panicking state a smidgeon.

My feet touched the wooden floor but I didn't trail far. Tremors quaked down my muscles. My gulping breaths came quick and sharp. A clammy sweat dewed my skin. Finn reached for me when he landed and I fell into his arms. The sob constricting my throat broke free and I didn't care if his affection for me right now was compelled. I needed him. I needed to feel safe.

"Rynnie love," he crooned into my hair over and over again, his breathing just as shaky as mine. Finn cupped my face with his hand, pressing me to his chest, and rested his cheek atop my head. The arm circling my waist pulled me in tighter. I couldn't get close enough to him. The sound of his thumping pulse sang to mine like a soothing lullaby. He had to be in pain after being my shield on the roof. Knowing that to be true, the tears flowed harder.

"I . . . I'm s-sorry," I stuttered in my tears.

"For being terrified?" he asked, confused. "We should be dead. Of course, you're upset."

I swallowed. "You didn't n-n-need to protect—"

"Taryn Hunt," he said my name so softly my heart cracked. The hand on my waist slid up my spine and began rubbing my upper back in gentle circles beneath my pack. "You are *not* a burden to me, lass. Caring for you is an honor I take seriously."

My eyes squeezed shut at his words. The swelling pressure in my chest was unbearable. I wanted so badly to believe his words. But he would sing a different song and dance if we lived long enough to bring all three objects to the witch. The moment our curse broke, everything would change.

If I were smart, I would push him away. But I couldn't. Not

this moment.

I melted into his warmth and safety and let him comfort me. And stars, he was so warm, almost hot to the touch. Was that magic? I drew in a deep breath and exhaled slowly. Inhaling deep once more, I focused on quieting my runaway fear and fell into the memory of his lips on mine, the feel of his breath kissing my skin, how those hands now holding me close had touched me with a reverence I had never experienced before. How, while un-dressed, this same warmth and comfort protected me at the inn. His bare skin had pressed to mine and not once did he take ad-vantage of my vulnerability. I didn't know what to do with that epiphany. I didn't know what to do—period.

Gently, Finn removed the small pack from my shoulders and shook out the blanket. "Come, lass," he whispered into my ear.

The affectionate sound of his voice spilled warmth down my trembling limbs and I almost started crying again. Finn lowered to the ground, pulling me down with him. He leaned his back on the ladder, then scooped me onto his lap. I curled up against his shoulder, burying into the strong arms holding me close, breath-ing in his mossy tree, spring rain, and cinnamon scent. When I settled, he wrapped the thin blanket around us.

Exhaustion tugged me toward sleep. But before I drifted away, I felt his lips pressed to my hair in a soft kiss as he whis-pered, "When I said I could fall for you, and fall hard, I didn't mean it literally."

I snorted.

For once, I appreciated how he smiled away the pain.

But stars, he was such an eejit.

"Goodnight, love," he whispered again, and I sank deeper into his warmth, not correcting that he called me love.

In the pitch black, with his arms holding me close, I could indulge in another Seren fantasy—I was his and he was mine. I never had to feel unsafe or unwanted again with him at my side. And in this fantasy, every feeling, every act of affection toward the other was real . . . not as fake nor as fleeting as our mate bond of convenience.

When we woke, I would need to put my shields back into place—for both our sake's. We could be friends, always. If he didn't resent me, that is. But we couldn't be lovers.

A fresh tear slipped down my cheek and followed me into restless sleep.

Chapter Sixteen

FINN BRANNON

Pain radiated from my side first. Fire rippled down my back next. The ladder rungs were digging into my spine My arms were stiff too. I didn't know how long we had slept in each other's arms. The attic didn't have any windows. But my body needed to move before I withered into an old, hunched over goblin.

Sorry, lass. These muscles for a bed needed to stretch.

I heaved a sigh and winced at a fresh wave of pain. Dark stars, I was probably bruised from the bird attacks too.

"You're wound is infected," Taryn murmured sleepily into my shoulder.

"It's fine—"

"Fussing about not fussing . . ." She nuzzled into my arm more. "Finny the Fusser."

Lips twitching, I patted the floor beside me for one of our shoulder bags. "You can fuss over my wound when we finish this job and not a moment sooner."

"You're such a stubborn arse."

My fingers curled around my satchel. Before leaving the inn, I took two candles and a box of matches from our room. The warehouses had enough natural light that candles weren't necessary. But in this attic? I would have lit one last night, but I didn't want to waste the limited resources we had when we were both passing out from shock and exhaustion.

Though, I wasn't sure if I wanted to know what fresh horror awaited us in this room. I had heard the scurry of rodents at one point in the night. The little whiskered beasties probably took off with what was left of our meager rations. I wanted to sigh, but that was the least of my worries today.

"Hold this." I handed Taryn one of the tallow tapers.

She slowly sat up and scooted off my lap with a yawn, and I was both aching for her to return and relieved to have full range of my limbs again. I struck a match and we both squinted at first. Taryn tilted her candle's wick toward the tiny flame. Once lit, she cupped her candle until I blew out the match, then held still as I lifted my wick to hers. Rustling around inside my bag again, I pulled out strips of my old shirt that I had planned to use as bandages, if needed. They *were* needed, but we couldn't have melted wax burn our hands either. Taryn took a strip and wrapped it near the base of her candle while I did the same to mine.

Amber painted her face in flickering light and shadow and highlighted strands of her dark hair in gold. The chaffed skin under her eyes had swelled red and her lips were dry and cracked. A low growl rumbled in my chest. My hands curled into fists. I would destroy the Thieves' Guilds for harming Taryn. But, right now, my lass needed water after crying herself to sleep. I only hoped I had enough left for her needs. I reached for my canteen, her guarded expression fixed on me the entire time.

"Drink," I said simply and pushed my water into her hand.

She narrowed her eyes. "How long has your wound been troubling you?"

"Doesn't change the present to know the unchangeable past." I dramatically pushed the canteen toward her face. "Drink or I'll bottle feed you like a wee *fussy* babe."

Taryn rolled her eyes but obeyed.

"Good girl."

Her adorable murder eyes threw knives at me as she drank. I arched a brow to keep up pretense, but she looked unwell. My fingers itched to caress her face and check the rest of her for any injuries from the bird attacks. I held back, though it killed me. If we had time to spare, I would suggest spending another day in the dark to rest. But we had seven days to steal the Eye of Lugh and find the Sisters Three before I had to return to Corbie. Though, I was starting to suspect that Corbie had already put a mark on me—on us.

A dizzy rush buzzed down my head and soured my empty stomach. I didn't need a mirror to know my skin was flushed, nor to feel my face to know it was clammy. Around the sundown before we started jumping rooftops, a fever had waxed and waned through my body. I tried not to worry. And didn't want to worry Taryn. The hag's curse may kill me eventually. Maybe Corbie would first.

Falling suns, I was on the edge of a pissy mood.

"I have another piece of the Maiden's riddle." Taryn's eyes lifted to mine. I sat up straighter, intrigued. "The Crone woke when *fifteen* magical objects were taken. Cursed us to only know *fifteen* feet of freedom. We borrowed *fifteen* days from a fae law to break this curse. I was *fifteen* the last I walked the walls of Stellar Wind. And, like the first time I tried to steal from this casino, I am . . . I am also free." She swallowed and focused on the candle's dancing flame. "This time, however, my freedom is cursed."

I slowly nodded. "As I said before, lass, the Sisters Three knew we were in Caledona Wood. They planned to curse us just so. The Amulet of Oisín was riddled to me. The Eye of Lugh is riddled to you."

"The Dobhar-chú tooth?"

"That, my wee otter wife," I said with a bittersweet smile, "is our monstrous fate, to fight *tooth* and nail for a romance—"

"Don't," she warned. "No romantic notions."

I ground my teeth together. A part of me knew she was battling the past. She was allowed her grief. But a cranky, soul weary, in-way-too-much-pain part of me was tired of her angry, biting wind. "Spit it out, lass. Nothing between us before we walk into another death trap."

She blinked back hot, swelling emotions. "You don't get to joke away all your pain and then demand to know mine."

My brows pushed together. "This is what ails you between us? That I'm not openly bitter about the shite hand life keeps dealing me?"

"There it is," she seethed. "The truth."

I growled, "What truth?!"

"That I am nothing more than a shite hand dealt to you!" The last words ended on a choke. "Would you hold me all night, through your pain, if we were not bound by ravens? Would you still make sure I was fed and warm and happy?"

"I am *not* him. I am *not* your parents." I leaned in closer to her, a few inches from her lips, and softened my voice. "You are not a burden to me, Taryn—"

"You are under a vow of magic to put me before all others!" Her hot breath caressed my mouth, my skin. "You are under the magic of your kind to provide for and protect your mate. Nothing about how you treat me is real!"

"Oh it is real, *love*." I drew out the forbidden word. The emotion that terrified her most. "Everything I do for you is real. I listen to the magic because you are worth it." Our mouths were nearly touching now. "I *want* to take care of you," I whispered hoarsely. "I *want* to protect you. And I would even if I didn't owe Corbie your bride price. I would even if we weren't bound as mates. You owe me nothing, Taryn Hunt. You are the best thing that has ever happened to me. Not a mistake. Not a regret." A furious tear crested her lashes and rolled down her cheek. "I can ignore my vows and fight our bond same as you. Damn the consequences." I leaned my forehead against hers and furiously whispered, "But I. Don't. Want. To."

"That, Finnan, is the cruelty of it all, isn't it? We both indulged in fantasies but we can't pine for a reality that will never be without breaking." Her words were quietly spoken, but they echoed in the dark as if shouted in an amphitheater. She sat back and drew in a hiccuped breath. "You will resent me when your primal magic no longer coerces your heart."

"Taryn—"

"No, Finnan Ó Brannon of Primry Green. Let go of the fantasies."

The air in my lungs constricted.

From the beginning, I had questioned if these feelings were real or the bond. If I would feel the same when our curse broke. But I knew the truth: she was fated to be mine. I sensed it from the moment of our curse.

But Taryn didn't want to hear about fate. Mortals grew skittish around the idea of forces beyond their understanding. The fae dabbled in magics and fates since our creation. I could feel it in my fevering blood, even now. The riddle of fifteen was no mere coincidence. The Sister Three knew we were in Caledona Wood—perhaps even orchestrating everything to ensure we were too.

Pining for a future we couldn't have while pretending we could was indeed a cruel trick, one that ached and writhed in my chest. The curse wasn't fifteen feet of freedom, it was a fifteen-foot gap we couldn't close fast enough. A collision of hearts that intensified as we emotionally drew farther apart.

I could scream and burn all Seren to ash right now.

A week ago, when waking beside her at the mineral spring, I had warned myself of the ripping pain I would know if I didn't protect myself against the mate bond's demands. A tearing grief I never wanted to experience again. An abandonment I feared with every breath.

I wasn't entirely sure when I began to think of Taryn as my mate truly. The inn perhaps? But when I kissed her and she kissed me back, I forgot that I had nothing, was nothing. That this was all temporary, a fantasy. The moment her lips touched mine, I owned the entire world.

She had become *everything* I had lost—my family, my home, my freedom.

And in another few days, I would lose her too.

This pain . . . this fecking pain was cracking me in two and I had only myself to blame. I knew better. I saw the warning signs and caved to those inner-puppy dog urges. I couldn't stop relentlessly panting after Taryn Hunt.

We held each other's eyes, neither she nor I able to conceal how desperately we wanted a whole life with each other while simultaneously rebuilding our walls. Stone by fated stone. Brick by cursed brick.

Then, because I knew it was what she expected, perhaps even wanted, a corner of my mouth lifted in a playful smirk. "Gather yourself, Rynnie," I said in a teasing voice, one that was awkwardly false, "before you frighten the all-*seeing* eye with the murderous red of yours."

Her shoulders relaxed. And then, because she knew it was also what I needed right now, she scoffed. "Not until you start quivering too. Fear me, Finn. Fear me."

"I'm afraid friends don't let friends fear being feared when there are far bigger things to fear than a small fearsome lass." I winked. "I'm a gent like that."

"The eejit just riddled away the last of his intelligence," she muttered. "His only virtue."

I shook my head. "I have my pretty face. The *only* virtue I need."

"Stars, your self-love has no shame."

"Absolutely none."

We smiled at one another—genuinely. How I loved this girl's grumpy wit. My heart continued to tear at the seams, knowing this would end soon, knowing Taryn would no longer be at my side, that I may not survive this hag's curse, but my soul felt a touch lighter. She didn't emotionally end things between us.

Still . . .

"Are we okay?" I asked, sobering. "I can't lose you, Taryn."

She studied my face. "You're stuck with my thieving ways, Finn. For as long as you'll have me as your friend."

"Good." My body slumped against the ladder rungs. "I don't bargain on potatoes for just anyone." I gestured with my candle at her. "Not to mention, you'd have to chain me up in a dungeon to stop me from taking care of you. So, no fussing."

Breaking eye contact, she watched a drip of wax slip down the taper to the cloth catch. "We better get moving," Taryn murmured, all business now. Her way of moving past emotionally uncomfortable situations. I didn't miss how the color drained some from her face, either.

As much as I ached for what could not be, I was glad she stole back some power in the place that had robbed her seven years ago.

Chapter Seventeen

FINN BRANNON

Stars, my muscles were on fire.

Slowly, I pushed to my feet, nearly toppling over when a dizzy spell hit me. As casually as possible, I gripped the ladder, hoping to not draw Taryn's attention. To hide the wincing pain radiating up my side, I lifted the candle and pretended to squint into the darkness.

Taryn stood, thankfully not noticing my struggles, and lifted her candle too.

And that's when I saw it.

A stuffed cow in the corner, its mouth opened in an eternal, silent moo. My own mouth hung open in a similar scream of horror. It wore a rat-chewed straw hat piled high with decorative fruits and vegetables. My eyes drifted downward and my jaw slackened even more. Its hooves were covered by red heeled dress boots and—I grimaced—a lacy pink garter teased high up its hind leg.

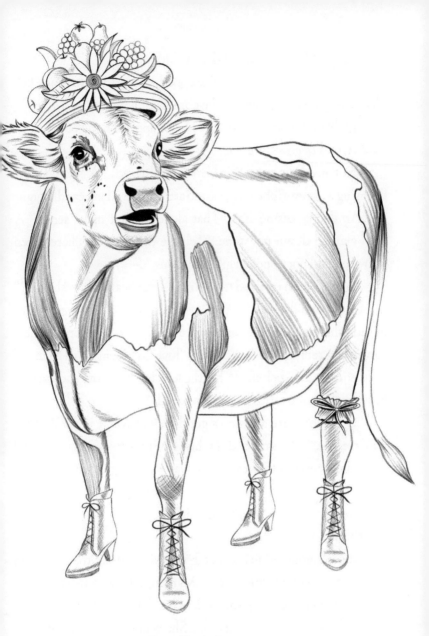

Cash Cow

Hear it's haunting moo and get
seven years bad luck.

"Why?" The only word that would form.

Taryn angled past me and stepped toward the hideous bovine, a slight scowl pinching the corners of her mouth.

I grabbed her arm. "No, lass. Do *not* approach the cow."

"Afraid of cows, are you?"

"Not just any cow, Rynnie." I shuddered. "A stuffed cow flaunting a garter ribbon in a casino attic." I lifted my candle higher. "An empty casino attic. That alone doesn't make sense." A chill clawed down my spine. "Tell me the cow was here seven years ago and not a special gift left for us."

At this, Taryn twisted to face me. "Ever heard of a cash cow?"

I slid her a flat look. "Aye, love. All the time. Favorite story us lads share to pass the long winter nights, it is." Her eyes narrowed in a reminder to not call her "love" while my eyes rounded in bewildered disbelief. "What the feck is a cash cow and exactly how many casino attics have you visited?"

"Cash cows are a casino's good luck charm. I was told they all have one." She grabbed my hand with a tremoring sigh and tugged me toward the cow. That was not going to happen. I dug in my heels. A laugh spurted past the stiff, pensive press of her lips. Her entire body was trembling.

Rynnie love . . .

Anger simmered just beneath my skin at what that male had done to her. Not just *him*, but the Maiden, who was also tormenting Taryn by demanding this task of her. The lass didn't need my protective fury right now, though. She needed a distraction.

"When you hear the cow's haunting moo chasing you in the bootlegger walls and earn seven year's bad luck, you will rue the time you spurred my keen, irresistibly attractive fae senses."

"Birds hit your head too many times, Finnan?" She scoffed, but the candle shook in her hand. "A pity your mystical faerie twinklings aren't irresistibly attractive enough to also detect hidden stairs to bootlegger walls."

My gaze shot to the cow and my shoulders fell. That abomination was a taxidermized scarecrow for raven thieves? Of course, it was. Whoever concocted the cash cow idea was a brilliant, sadistic arse. Reluctantly, I followed Taryn and tried not to recoil. How Taryn could was a mortal strength I envied. Fae kind were far too superstitious for our own good sometimes. *Good luck charm, my arse.*

Taryn knelt on the ground and reached up into the cow's udders. Her brows scowled in concentration as she felt around. A couple of seconds later, she lifted a tiny crowbar from between the udders and I nearly gagged. I didn't even want to know how it was affixed to that dressed up attic creature of nightmares.

"This scares you but not a cottage full of skunk ornaments?"

"Witches turn people into animals all the time. It's what they do," I answered with a shrug. "This is unnatural. And," I added with a grimace, "none of those skunks wore garter ribbons. I will never see that feminine underpinning again and not think of this fecking cow. I could weep for days."

She groaned—again—this time pulling a mild look of disgust. "Stop your gobshiting and get down here."

My head swam in dizzy circles, but I joined her on the floor. Pain flared around my middle and up my back and I sucked in a sharp breath. Realizing my mistake, I quickly straightened and put on a brave face.

Taryn thrust her candle into my hand with a pointed look. What in the dark stars did she think I was going to do?—

Oh.

She was pissed about my hag-cursed wound secret.

Well, she still hadn't shared *his* name, so we were even.

Blowing a strand of hair from her eyes, she plopped a floorboard up directly beneath the cow's belly with the crowbar. Followed by two more. And sure enough, there was a ladder leading down a narrow shaft in the wall.

"Ready?" She took her candle from my outstretched hand with white-knuckling fingers.

The shake in her voice snapped the protective puppy dog inside of me to attention. I was on the verge of growling a demand for her to tell me his name.

"Go," she said, her voice tight. "I'll put the crowbar and floorboards back."

I swallowed back the growing queasiness. I wasn't sure if that was the infection or foreboding. There was a very real chance we may not survive. We had better odds against the Dobhar-chú than nicking the Eye of Lugh and making it to the mainland while still breathing.

Sighing, I crawled beneath the belly of the beast.

Chapter Eighteen

TARYN HUNT

There was maybe four feet of width between the real and false walls, both made of brick. Trash and old rats' nests littered the floor. I tried not to think about it too much or jump when we startled rodents into the walls.

A tremor was picking up speed. Sweat dewed my forehead and my hands were growing clammy. Memories flashed into my mind with every step. His beautiful dark purple eyes inviting me to trust him—so dark, they were nearly as black as the feathery mussed tresses that fell to his brows. Silky strands of hair that reflected blue in the light. And his voice, stars . . . just thinking about the soft, melodic sound still sent chills down my spine seven years later. Was that just his coercion magic?

I was fifteen, almost sixteen, and believed myself in love.

He was the most beautiful male I had ever beheld. We had planned a home, children, owning a shop together. Everything I had wanted.

Still wanted . . . but now with an entirely different faerie boy I also wouldn't have after robbing Stellar Winds Casino.

Finn and I had been traveling down passageways for around twenty minutes now. The last time I was here, it was to rob cash vaults with hidden access from the bootlegger walls. I didn't know where to go for this job. Peep holes were placed every ten feet or so. A few places had levers to open hidden doors in the false wall with sliding mechanics. So far, we had passed a gentlemen's room for high bidders, private chambers for the Night Doves of Seren's casinos to satisfy their buyers, but no offices. Eventually the passageway would lead to stairs to travel along the main gambling floors. But I continually paused on the word "tower" of Corvus Rook. Wherever the Eye was, it had to be on this upper level.

Finn remained silent, but I could feel his excitement. Why traveling through bootlegger walls was so thrilling to him, I'd never understand. I casually peered over my shoulder and met his eyes. He arched a pointed brow at me. Heaving stars, he was so pale, his skin appearing as clammy as my hands felt. But the barest hint of a smile played across his lips.

I faced forward and kept moving.

A few steps later, I heard a strange moaning sound. The hair on my arms rose. Was someone hurt? Did a crime boss keep a traitor in these halls? My heart was racing, my eyes darting to every shadow. I was about to twist toward Finn to see if he heard it too when the sound reached my ears again.

"Mooooooo . . ."

Friends, the murder in my eyes traveled straight to my fists in a lightning flash. Do *not* mourn the lad.

I spun on my heels so fast, he startled back a step. Finn didn't even try to hide his smug delight at my anger. Baring my teeth, I swung and he jumped out of the way.

"Put some effort into it, Rynnie," he mocked, though his eyes were strangely soft and protective.

But I only saw red. Careful not to drop my candle, I threw another punch, this one landing him square in the chest. A growl left me and I punched him again. He stood still and let me, too. Angry tears gathered on my lashes. I couldn't stop hitting him.

"Tell me his name."

"Because you moo'd at me?" I pounded on his chest again with a quiet guttural scream. "What in the stars damned sky is wrong with you, Finn Brannon?" I whispered harshly.

Finn grabbed my wrist, then pressed the palm of my hand to his heart, covering my fingers with his. "His name, lass."

"Ren Cormac!" I seethed. "Are you happy now?"

The already sickly shade of Finn's skin grew more bloodless. "His name is Raven, Son of Raven . . ."

Fear crept up my spine. "What are you talking about?"

"'Ren' is a nickname in my fae tongue for raven." Finn swallowed thickly. "And 'Cor' is short for Corb, also raven in my tongue, and 'mac' means son."

My heart dropped to my stomach. "You're saying he's . . . an actual raven?"

"A Raven Folk."

I was going to be sick. "As in a shifter?"

"Black hair with blue cast, dark eyes, pale skin? A lyrical, almost musical rhythm to his speech?"

"Yes," I breathed in growing disgust.

"Raven son of . . . " he murmured. Our eyes locked. "The raven son of Corvus Rook most likely."

I stumbled back a horrified step. The son of the Thieves' Guild boss had tricked me. I wrapped my arm around my gut. Did he trick other girls into Black Beak and Corbie, or worse? I shuddered thinking how I could have become a dove. I hadn't seen him since I was arrested. Had he followed me in a raven form, though?

I peered up at Finn and froze. The pure canined fury on his face, the slitted fire in his eyes, he was terrifying. It was easy to forget that he was a creature. All fae were. But I knew little about the wild fae. The animalistic, predatory way he locked onto the darkness over my shoulder shivered down my body.

And, in that spooked moment, a thought hit me. Brann was a common name for boys on Seren, which translated to raven in a different fae tongue. My pulse kickstarted into a gallop.

"Your surname," I whispered. The angry heat of his gaze slid to mine. "Are you Raven Folk?"

"No," he answered in a low growl. "The Caravan fae who took me in were."

Perhaps I was foolish to approach him when he was more beast than not, but I returned my hand to his chest. Finn would never hurt me. Seeing him in a more primal state, though? Delicious warmth buzzed down the entire length of me, the sparking embers settling low in my belly. This fierceness had kissed me, passionately. Had wanted to make me his. Would this very moment if I asked him to. Stars, my blood blushed hot, a flush of longing I needed to shove away. But it was difficult to when his possessive gaze lingered on my lips before slowly meeting my eyes.

We weren't friends before all this. We were terrible at being friends now.

"Your wild fae name?" I asked breathlessly, pushing back the ache.

"Fionnán Ó Dair."

While this wasn't his True Name, I didn't expect him to actually tell me his family's. "Finnan of the . . ." I started to translate.

"Fair One of the Oak.'"

"You're a tree spirit?" My lips parted.

A corner of his mouth hooked up. "Something like that."

I thought back to our time in Caledona Wood, how his beauty was amplified when surrounded by the greens of trees and ferns. I knew little about the wild fae, but I knew they were elemental nature spirits. I could see it now, a forest dweller folk formed from the magic of earth and trees. Being ripped from his family, his very roots, forced to wander then thieve on an unnatural, factory-built island . . . my heart ached deeply for him. Now I understood why he could more easily smile away his pain. Beneath it all, he was as strong and sturdy as an oak, with a nature made to better weather life's storms.

Finn's pale eyes watched me take him in anew—eyes the color of unfurling new spring leaves.

My lips pressed into a line. "I thought your name meant 'handsome' not 'fair colorings.'"

He started quietly laughing, then angled past me with a wink.

Holding back a frustrated sigh, I followed him down the next corridor. "Did you consider Corvus or Rook to be Raven Folk?"

"I never really considered what fae they were. Many of my kind command ravens. The birds are attracted to us and us to them. It has always been."

"But their names."

"Aye," he said with a single nod of his head. "I believed them street names to match the guilds, nothing more, nothing less. They still could be."

A rat scurried over my boot and I held back a squeak. I couldn't get out of these walls fast enough—

Finn halted his steps. A preternatural stillness fell over his body. I was about to ask him what had his hackles up when he lifted his candle higher. On the ceiling was a crude painting of a cow. "This is a trap," he whispered.

"Tell me, Finn, what hasn't been a trap since we were assigned to catch the weather ring?"

He twisted toward me. "The ravens saw us lower into the attic. They know we're here. Easier to arrest us in the building proper—" Finn's words cut off in a grimacing flinch. He sucked in a sharp breath and touched his side. "Shite," he breathed. My fingers flew to his shirt, but he grabbed my wrist. "After the job."

"Can you even do this job?" I shot back. Beads of sweat gathered on his forehead and my pulse began spinning.

He lowered his face until we were eye level. "After. The. Job."

"Don't be ridiculous."

He pushed my hand back toward me, drawling, "Ravish me later—"

"You let me hit you, you arse!" I cried out in a loud whisper.

"Darling kitten punches, my feisty forest cat." He blinked innocently at me and stepped back. "Plus, you needed to hit a boy who had promised you his heart. Now," he said, gesturing to the ceiling with his head, "we need a plan."

"Oh, aye, you think? Smart one you are, Ó Dair."

He grinned. "Ó Dair when you want to strangle me but not murder me?"

"And rearrange your balls."

His rascally grin melted into sensual lines and I rolled my eyes.

"So, former Caravan thief of the Raven Folk," I said on an exasperated sigh, "if I were the boss of a Thieves' Guild and I knew two thieves were after my magical all-*seeing* bird Eye, where would I hide it?"

"Raven Folk are tricksters. Their arrogance finds amusement in hiding a powerful object in the open under an illusion spell while crowing in delight as the fools get fooled." Finn shrugged, as if that were an obvious answer. "Most thieves would look for vaults or under the mattress. Raven Folk would hide a decoy there and glamour it to look like the target object."

Just lovely.

"Does anything reveal illusion spells?"

"Smoke and mirrors, Rynnie love." In one pointed look, he dared me to challenge him on reverting back to street slang, but I was too tired to care. "Smoke to drive out the hidden spell and a mirror to reveal the alternate reality. It takes artful deception to reveal other crafted deceptions."

Of course, it did. The fae and their stars damned riddles. But I was in the mood for this one.

"Smoke, you say, Finny love?" I lifted my candle, a vindictive curl to my lips. "Then let's burn this fecking building to the ground."

Chapter Nineteen

TARYN HUNT

I balanced on Finn's shoulders, who knelt on the ground while holding both candles. Cross beams stretched from the false wall to the real one, but not where the cow was painted. Carefully, I popped a board up just enough to peep above the lip of the floor in search of shoes and winced. The loud, rattling sound of birds in cages scraped at my ears. Was this a rookery?

I lifted the plank just a smidgeon higher.

Slivers of light burned my eyes, something I should have expected after living in barely lit darkness for who knows how long. I squinted and blinked until adjusted enough to do a quick sweep. Legs of furniture. Rugs. My gaze landed on one pair of shoes to the right; the owner shifted on his feet. Straight ahead was another pair of shoes with a toe tapping an impatient rhythm.

"Two," I whispered down to Finn.

I lowered the plank, then eased down Finn's shoulders.

Rising to a stand, he reached out to the wall to steady himself. Those beautiful pale green eyes were starting to look glassy. But, in typical Finn fashion, he tossed me a sideways smile. He didn't want me to fuss, but he was growing sicker. Faster than was normal for an infection on a wound that had mostly healed up. I would make a stand until he was forced to tell me what was going on, but we didn't have time to wait out his stubbornness.

"Let's slip into a dove's chamber," I said.

Finn gestured with his head to lead the way.

If we popped in from the bootlegger entry, we'd have no advantage against any guards or even Corvus Rook. So we'd walk in the front door . . . after setting the hallway on fire. And lighting rooms we pass through too. Flames on upper levels were not only harder to put out, it would also make it harder for others to reach us. And that target room was on the same level as the attic. Stairs from inside had to lead there. We'd either tie drapes into knots and lower ourselves from the window or use the bootlegger walls to escape through another part of the casino—an unlit part.

Backtracking down the passageway, we passed the first set of pleasure chambers. If they were occupied, I had no idea, nor did I want to. We were specifically looking for one with a hidden sliding door.

"There." Finn pointed ahead. I jogged to the peep holes and peered in. "Anything?" Finn whispered behind me.

"No," I confirmed. "Should we wait a minute or two just to make sure?"

"We need to keep moving," he said. But I heard what he was really saying: he didn't know how long he would last. My heart jumped to my throat. "Taryn," he warned. "Don't look at me like that, love."

"Then tell me——"

He pulled the lever, his eyes locked onto mine. Gears above the door began spinning and, with a hiss, the hidden door unlocked and Finn slid it open. Cool afternoon light poured into the passageway and both me and Finn instinctually lifted our hands to shield our eyes. Stars, it was annoying. Before walking into the room, he blew out his candle, then mine. We would re-light as needed. The contents of his pack were now in mine and old rats' nests and flammable garbage were stuffed into his along with a book of matches.

We crept into the room and quietly jogged to the chamber door. Finn peeked out this time. Males leaving these rooms weren't uncommon. But I wasn't dressed as a Night Dove.

"Clear," he whispered over his shoulder. Opening the door wider, he moved into the hallway. "Shite!" he swore. "Employees." The clomp of bootsteps echoed down the hall. Finn spun back toward me. "Pull me back in and sound flirtatious." His head angled toward the source of the footfalls and he lifted a smirk in greeting.

Despite Finn's teasing, the ability to seduce was low on my skill set. I didn't know the first thing about being flirtatious.

"Taryn," he growled under his breath.

Glaring, I drawled in a flat, deadpanned voice, "Hey big boy." His brows shot up. When the shock wore off a half-second later, he sputtered a low laugh. I mechanically stuck my arm out and fisted his shirt. In the most wooden, lackluster voice I could conjure, I asked, "Where do you think you're going, pointy ears?"

Performance of the century, friends. *How do I seduce you now, Finny?*

The bootsteps grew louder. I could hear two men chuckling in conversation with each other.

To hide me from sight, Finn fell forward, as if I had tugged him, and stopped just short of entering, his mouth still twisted in barely suppressed laughter. Dark green strands fell over his eyes in a deliciously boyish look and my breath fluttered.

"I think I love you, Taryn Hunt," he whispered with a humored smile.

Before I could react, he cupped my face and slammed his mouth onto mine.

I stopped breathing.

I stopped thinking.

His lips possessed mine in a claiming that reached through my rising panic, past the fortressed walls around my bruised heart, clear to my terrified soul.

Love me?

The voices were almost upon us. One of the men made a crude comment and, if it were any other situation, I would be mortified. Not missing a beat, Finn broke our kiss long enough to wink in their direction, then captured my lips again while walking me backward, kicking the door closed behind him.

I thought he would stop then. The show was over.

But his kiss slowed to a sensual tempo, his tongue teasing mine in a way so provocative, it felt like he was undressing me with each stroke. My fingers dug into his chest. The memory of caressing his bare skin pleasurably shivered down me. One of his hands lightly trailed down my neck to trace the curve of my breast, the curve of my waist and hip. Moon and stars, I was growing delirious under his touch. Deepening our kiss, he moaned, a heady, drunk sound, and liquid fire ignited my melting pulse.

I wanted to run far away. I wanted to press in even closer. To hear him say he loved me over and over until his voice grew hoarse. To tell him I loved him too and would until my dying breath. To pull him onto the bed behind us and finish what we started the other night. To shove him away and scream as my heart shattered to dust.

Finn's body recoiled in a wince. A tight, strangled sound he breathed into our kiss.

I jumped back, eyes wide. But his hand continued to cradle my face.

His skin was so pale. Why was he this sick?

Before I could challenge him again, or rebuild the walls he just demolished, he murmured, "I have nine hundred and ninety-six more kisses to steal from you." Finn pressed his lips to mine again, a soft, sweet kiss that ached down to the tip of my toes. "Nine hundred and ninety-five."

Dropping his hands from my body, he turned toward the large, canopied bed.

I watched in bewildered fascination as he first stripped a sheet from the bed, wadded it up and threw at me to keep for our possible through-the-window escape, then placed a patch of old rats' nest on a pillow and struck a match. Bending, he gently blew onto the smoking material until it crackled into a hungry flame. Then he pulled me from the room once confirming the hallway was clear.

We didn't talk about what just happened as we stuck to the shadows and moved in and out of rooms—I now held onto four sheets. But he didn't shy away from me either, sliding me little smiles here and there. A few hours ago, we agreed to only act as friends. And now he was confessing love and stealing kisses again. Dread tightened in my gut. A niggling thought I refused to give any attention to the sicker he appeared.

Still, I couldn't shake his confessions from the attic. Or the tender, protective way he looked at me since traveling the bootlegger walls.

What if everything he said was true?

What if he really could ignore the magic of our mate bond and was still choosing me like I chose him?

What if I embraced the pain of losing Finn to soak up every moment of possessing him now?

I didn't think I would survive the heartbreak of separation. I couldn't remain in Seren with him. Corbie—no, Ren and his family—would trick me into enslavement again and it would add to Finn's debts. If it meant I could free Finn, I would deal with Ren. But I wouldn't steal away more of Finn's freedom.

Now was all we had.

Now was all we may ever have.

Here's the lesson, mainlanders . . . don't throw rocks at unnaturally pretty elven males in front of a witch's cottage unless you're willing to marry his arrogant, thieving arse. Bonus emotion: a willingness to eternally ache to be forever attached at his hip while wanting to punch that ridiculously beautiful face for making you fall for a life you can only have with him for a few stolen days. Additional perk: angry pining.

Cursed stars, how I angry pined for him.

We quickly lit whatever we could on fire as we moved toward where stairs had to lead to the so-called tower. Every corner I turned, every empty room I entered, I lived in fear of coming face to face with Ren or Corvus Rook. There were moments I wanted to vomit from the intensity of nerves twisting in my middle.

Behind us, screams and shouts warning, "Fire," finally began to echo down the hall.

A door crashed open beside us and I nearly startled into Finn's arms. We had just lit the room next over. Scantily clad girls and men in fancy suits with top hats poured into the hallway, too panicked to notice how out of place Finn and I looked for this casino let alone by one of several gentlemen's club rooms. Maybe they thought I was a maid, since I was carrying a wad of bedding in my arms?

We pressed to the wall next to the door, opposite of their stampeding escape, waiting . . . waiting . . . My pulse pounded in my ears. Smoke curled from the open door and I swallowed thickly. More screams reached us from ten or so yards away. Finn's lips tilted in satisfaction.

When the hall appeared empty, Finn nodded to follow him. We crept into the vacated room and strode directly to the first gaming table. Finn wiggled his eyebrows at me, then scooped up a hefty pile of abandoned mainlander money and stuffed it into my pack. He grabbed even more money and shoved it in his pockets followed by mine.

"For your apothecary shop," he said, kissing my forehead.

Oh my stars . . .

Tears brimmed my lashes. My heart swelled with joy and cracked in half simultaneously. Finn started to turn toward the door and I yanked him back to me. His questioning gaze snapped to mine and, before I lost all bravery, I dropped the sheets, wrapped my hands around his neck, and . . . stole my first kiss from him.

Everything he did, he did for me. Even though my mortal life was short compared to his. Even while the world burned around us, while he was sick and in pain, he was protecting my future and making sure I was cared for in his absence.

A sob knotted in my chest.

Furious tears over how I had been too afraid to accept his affection as real and now our time together was almost up.

Raging tears, each one a promise to make Ren and Corvus Rook pay for stealing our happiness, stealing our freedom.

I refused to have a life without Finn by my side. It was unimaginable at this point. We were partners in crime, he and I. Whatever it took to keep him, I would find a way.

Our kiss slowed and he opened his eyes to search mine.

"I think I love you, Finn Brannon."

He smiled against my lips, a cocky grin just to taunt me. He already knew—the eejit. "You told me no more pity swoons."

"You agreed to just be my friend."

"No I didn't."

"You—" Dammit. He didn't. It was a-marriage-in-name-only bargaining fail all over again. I huffed a humored, irritated sigh.

The corner of his mouth lifted higher. "Ready to pull off the greatest heist in Seren history, my wee murderous thieving potato?"

I snorted. "Let's out trick a tricksome trickster trickily."

"Oh, love," he crooned, biting his lower lip. He didn't have to finish. I knew what was on the tip of his tongue. *Yeah, Finny boy, I speak your love language.* I winked at him, scooped up the sheets, then waltzed out the door, knowing he was right on my tail, a stupid smirk on his stupidly handsome face.

Hand in hand, we jogged down the smoke-filled hall. People fled from rooms we passed in frantic droves, both patrons and casino employees. But none in the direction we ran, or seemed to care that we were moving upstream against the pandemonium.

After wending down a side hall, we rounded a corner and . . . the corridor ended at a window.

"Feck!" I hissed.

Nothing seemed to lead toward the tower room. Finn's glassy eyes darted around, studying the walls, the floor, nearby doors. A scowl pinched between his brows; his lips dipped into a frown. I paced the floor, my gaze hunting for clues. An ornate rug covered the wooden floors. Gray and cream pinstriped wallpaper lined the walls above ebony wainscoting. Paintings were artfully hung down the hall, from still life to pastoral scenes—I sucked in an excited breath.

"Finn!" I tugged on his arm then pointed.

On the wall across from a door was an oil painting of a cow donning a straw hat, one that stood beside a pair of red heeled shoes tossed onto a picnic blanket next to a basket of fruit.

Excited, we opened the door and took in another gentle-man's room. Were there so many wealthy males that a half-dozen high-bidder gambling rooms were needed? *Gods . . .*

"Let's go," he urged, practically pushing me into the room and shutting the door behind us.

We quickly piled furniture as a shield wall at the entrance. Then we pulled the drapes from the windows and lit them on fire against the doors.

"Candles," he commanded simply. "There's a mirror in my belongings too."

I arched a brow, humored. "I knew you were in love with yourself, but even that's excessive."

He plucked the objects from my hand with a humored snort and busied with lighting the candles again while my gaze roamed the back wall for a clue. Finn sidled beside me, handing me a can-dle. "Ready to walk through walls?"

"Magical faerie twinkling nudges, is it?"

"You forgot 'irresistibly attractive.'" He lifted the mirror and kissed at his reflection—and froze. Dark circles were lining his eyes and a clammy flush dewed his sickly pale skin. Clenching his jaw, he lowered the mirror and marched over to the back wall. "Don't look at me like that, Rynnie."

"Then tell me what's going on."

As expected, Finn ignored me and turned, his shoulder to the wall as he began walking a straight line. He placed his candle near the paisley printed wallpaper and angled the mirror to see the smoking reflection. We walked slowly, Finn moving the candle up and down every so often. At the end, he growled low and frantically peered around the room. A second later his nose wrinkled in a mild look of disgust. I followed his gaze and burst into laughter. On a perpendicular wall, one covered in knick-knacks and odd-end paintings, was a single pink garter ribbon strung from the low ceiling.

"Weeping," he muttered while approaching the section of wall below the pink lace garter. Lifting the candle and mirror, a slow smile spread on his face. I gasped. In the mirror's smoky reflection, the curio cabinet filled with crystal figurines disappeared into an open doorway. Behind this wall was another bootlegger hall. Finn stuck his arm through the illusion and started to walk through when I pulled him back.

"Wait." There was a real chance I might see Ren or Corvus Rook in the tower. "Coerce me," I croaked.

"What?" Finn's eyes widened. "Taryn, I don't think—"

"Can you coerce me to listen only to your commands until you end the spell?"

Understanding softened his face. Taking the sheets from my hand, he dropped them on the floor, then handed me his candle and the mirror. Slowly, he cupped my cheeks and I drew in a shaky voice. "You trust me not to harm you."

It was a statement, not a question. "The other two times were only to protect me?"

"I swear to you, Taryn."

I swallowed back against the painful grit in my throat. "Then make this time no different."

Finn drew closer to me, until our lips almost touched, and

spoke, "Mate." The single word warbled in my head. A single word filled with so much pleasure, I felt my blood blush. "You will only obey my command or your own. I do not take away your will," he whispered, "but no other will be allowed to coerce you but me."

He dropped his hands.

"Mate," I repeated softly. Warmth filled my chest in a way I hadn't allowed until now.

"Aye, you are mine, Taryn Brannon Ó Dair," Finn said, a crack in his voice, "*Mine*. There is no future where this will never not be true for me. Even though I want you to find love and happiness, open your shop, and have all the children you desire. Even though I may never see you again after our curse is broken. Even though our marks will disappear. You will always be my wife, my mate."

Taryn Brannon Ó Dair.

Finn brushed his lips across mine. "Nine hundred and ninety-four."

Then he disappeared into the wall and took my heart with him.

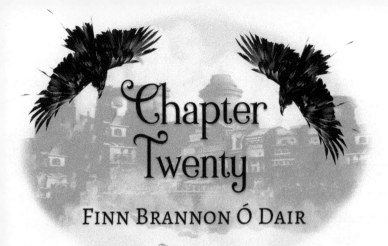

Chapter Twenty

FINN BRANNON Ó DAIR

Every breath sent sharp daggers to my cursed wound. It was an effort to remain unaffected. I was starting to lose my grip. Dizziness circled my head from an ever-present fever. But I wasn't as worried as I could be this moment.

Knowing Raven Folk like I did, I would be surprised if Ren Cormac or Corvus Rook were in the tower room waiting for us. And I had a feeling the Eye of Lugh was still up there too. We were petty thieves in their eyes. Ones that were occasionally sent to the mainland for bigger jobs. Not ones who were conniving enough to find this room let alone orchestrate and pull off a heist like this.

We had caught them by surprise. Every move. Every action.

No, they wouldn't be up there while their "nest" was on fire—they didn't know to plan for a fire. Unless they had an entrance by air for their raven forms, we had blocked their only access. With a blaze below us, we needed to act fast. I banked on the unfolding chaos to conceal our escape. The more bodies gathered on the streets, the better for us. I only hoped the ferries weren't overbooked as a result.

Taryn jogged up a narrow set of stairs behind me. Falling suns, all I wanted to do was push her up against a wall and lose my soul to her lips, worship every tantalizing line and curve of her body, memorize the dance of her breath as she came undone beneath me. A lad could dream.

Alas . . .

At the top of the stairs, I closed my eyes and drew in a fortifying breath. I mentally focused on my street brawling skills to reassure the dread pinching my gut. The two guards Taryn saw, if still there, were probably armed. Better to have the element of surprise than give them a warning by trying to sneak in.

"Stand back," I reminded Taryn. Then, with my hand on the knob, I slammed open the door.

A male guarding the entrance didn't hesitate a single breath and sprang into action. But I was faster, anticipating someone this close to the entry. My fist swung up and connected to his jaw in a solid crunch. His head snapped back. Baring my teeth, I crushed his windpipe in a swift strike while his body still wobbled from the upper cut. He collapsed to the floor, critically choking. I gave him two- or three-minutes tops.

Sweat dripped down my forehead. Just that low amount of action tipped my strength upside down. The room tilted for a moment and I stumbled back a step. Like when a Black Beak lad had hit my head in a tumble after I stole his catch—I won. I would win this next round too. My mate's safety depended on it.

Taryn shouted my name.

The second male charged me with a knife. Despite my momentary disorientation, I lifted my fists in a boxer's stance. A knife fight made the odds far less in my favor. But a lad didn't grow up in Seren's warehouse district without learning how to fight dirty.

I lifted my fists a touch higher and—

The male pitched sideways and crashed into a bird cage housing two ravens. The birds cawed obscenities. I almost laughed at their creative swears, but I was confused. What the hell just happened? My gaze jumped to Taryn, who was gaping at the fallen male, a sickly hue to her paling skin. Then I saw it. An orb on the ground, rolling toward us. Or whatever it really was beneath the illusion spell.

"You were aiming for the window again, weren't you, lass?" I asked in a serious voice, though I wasn't serious.

Her horrified expression melted into dry humor. "Still pissed about that, are you?"

"Rule one, Rynnie," I replied with a mock-tsk. "The most important rule of all, it is. I seek justice, naturally."

She studied the man she hit, her mouth opening with what was undoubtedly another sarcastic reply, but then it closed and her eyes widened. The room pulled into sharper view.

Feck. Me.

At least fifteen gilded cages dotted the room, each one filled with one or two spy ravens. Their sudden loud chatter clawed at my ears. Too many were talking at once to make out their conversation too. My eyes darted around to quickly take in the rest of the room. Late afternoon sun filtered through the draped windows and reflected off fifty or more illusioned dark orbs the size of a small bowl, each one artistically displayed around the room on pedestals, on bookshelves, and other various furniture pieces. The orbs were probably broken fountain pens, chipped teacups, a clogged up tobacco pipe, and other odd-end junk.

Well, this couldn't get worse than our experience on the rooftop, so . . .

"Evening, ladies and gents," I greeted with a lazy bow. The ravens continued to chatter amongst each other again.

"Fire."

"He could save us."

"I don't trust him."

"We need to escape."

"Fire, fire, fire."

"The Maiden."

"Let's bargain."

My ears perked at that last comment.

"Aye," I said, "we'll bargain with you. Who's in charge here?"

One raven quietly cawed from the center. "Finn Brannon, I seek your protection."

I pushed forward and grit back another flare of pain. I didn't trust the other ravens, but I unlocked his cage and he flew to my outstretched hand. "What do you want?"

The raven cawed. "Set us free and we won't sound the alarm."

I relayed the bargain to Taryn, whose large doe eyes whipped to mine. Dark, earthen brown flyaway strands from her loosened, waist-length braid fell around her face, setting off the light olive tones of her skin. A scratch along her hairline, one I hadn't previously noticed, snagged my gaze and the protective puppy dog in me snarled to attention.

"Before I agree," I growled low, teeth bared. "Anyone here harm my mate last night on the roof?"

The raven cawed again.

My shoulders slumped. "I can't hold that against you, lad."

"Why are they innocent?" Taryn whispered at my side.

"Coerced." I studied the metal anklet around the raven's foot. "The tags are linked to the Eye."

She placed a fisted hand on her hip and cocked her head. "How do we know they're not lying to us? They could attack us the moment—"

The birds all began flapping their wings in the cages and I raised my free hand. "Calm your lovely ruffled feathered breasts." To her, I explained, "Ravens are one of the last lines of old fae. They're incapable of lying. It's why our mate bonds are made in their magic."

"I know one raven who lied to me," she snapped in reply.

"Raven Folk are shifters, not ancient fae." I shrugged, a combination of were-you-not-paying-attention and mortals-have-adorable-simple-brains.

"Fine," she sighed and gestured around the room. "Do they know which one is the Eye of Lugh?"

The head raven cawed.

I slid her a side-long glance. "One of the dark orbs, he says."

"Why didn't I think of that?" she replied, equally as mock

serious.

The raven cawed again.

"He says, 'you're welcome.'" My lips twitched.

Taryn arched a brow at . . . G90K the tag read. "This is my bargain. I will agree to set you and your old fae friends free if you lead us to the Eye of Lugh."

"Not just a legendary beauty after all," I playfully jabbed with a smirk. Her dark eyes narrowed into promises to turn me inside out and my impish smile widened. Returning my attention to the raven, I said, "We accept your bargain to free you if you agree to lead us to the Eye of Lugh first and not alarm Corvus or Rook or Corvus Rook or anyone under the employ of or associated with the name Corvus or Rook at any point now or later, aye?"

"Aye, we agree Finn Brannon."

The raven alighted into the air from my hand and flew to a wild "purse leaf" variety of fern in a porcelain cow-shaped planter by the window. I tilted my head. Well, wasn't that clever. I lifted the candle to curl smoke around the plant and angled the mirror. A dark purple, almost black orb with raven feathers swirling within reflected back to us instead of a cow and fern. An orb that looked identical to the decoys illusioned around the room.

"The cash cow," I said to Taryn.

She grinned, a wicked sort of grin that shot heat straight to my groin. Seven moons, she was killing me faster than this hag's curse.

Shooing the raven away, she plucked the Eye from the marble pedestal it was on and stuffed what looked like a small potted fern into her bag—and would until we could break the illusion. She then turned to the room. "Stick your tagged foot out of the cage. No one is set free until all the tags are snipped. You will *not* attack me again. If you do, I'll pluck your feathers one by one until you're nothing but a sad, bald pigeon, understand?"

The birds all quickly complied. I didn't blame the poor wee souls. She frightened me too . . . when Taryn chose violence, I feared I couldn't fall to my knees fast enough to receive my punishment. She really did make it difficult to want to be good.

Using my pocketknife, I quickly began to remove the tags. Taryn cracked the nearest window open a few inches. With a nod from her, I began unlatching cage doors. She flinched when the first few birds flew past her. When the last of the birds escaped, she shut the window to ensure a Raven Folk didn't slip in while we turned the four bedsheets into ropes.

We worked beside each other in silence—a heavy celebratory silence.

All three objects were now in our possession. The only task remaining was to reach the mainland and locate the Sisters Three without Corvus Rook stopping us first.

I tied the end of our makeshift rope to a large ebony wood desk, the largest, heaviest object in the room. Blowing out a shaking breath, I tugged on the sheets to ensure the knot was secure. "I'll go first."

She swallowed but nodded her head.

I reopened the window and hopped onto the sill, ignoring the woozy spinning in my head. If I stopped to kiss her or cut open more of my heart to bleed at her feet, I wouldn't leave this room. My body was fighting to remain present. And, so, with a dip of my head, I walked backward down the brick wall before my body gave out.

Knifing pain seared my middle and clamped the muscles of my chest. A strangled cry left my lips. I needed to hold on and push through. If I fell, the magic would force us back together. A collision thirty feet above the ground would be fatal.

Taryn eased back onto the wall and my pulse jumped. I couldn't protect her right now. I had to trust she had the strength to rappel herself down this wall. At least if she fell, I would land beneath her and hopefully cushioned the impact enough that she might survive.

Syncing to her rhythm, I lowered bit by bit. Sweat poured into my eyes. My muscles shook. I clenched my jaw so hard, I thought my teeth might crack. When we finally reached the ground, I was near to passing out. Taryn placed my arm over her shoulders and I didn't fight her. I was truly weak.

Thick smoke covered the alley, hiding our forms. I coughed, sending hot daggers to my side. A small cry passed my lips. We quickly emerged from the alley and melted into a large crowd. A bucket brigade had formed from a prominent fountain on the edge of Crescent Street to Stellar Winds Casino. People didn't notice us as we angled past. And, if they did, their stares didn't linger long.

Windows shattered behind us. The crowd collectively gasped. Several panicked and pushed into the crowd. I darkly chuckled, a strained, breathy sound. I hoped the arsehole never recovered.

"Kalen!" Taryn called out. She hollered his name and waved a hand.

My best mate jogged up to us and recoiled. "Stars, Finn . . ." He grabbed my face, his eyes wide. "Where?" he asked. I think Taryn pointed to my side. I was struggling to remain conscious. "I can smell the curse on you, mate. It decays in your blood." Kalen's voice was frantic. He touched my side and I recoiled with a sharp hiss. "We need to find a witch—"

"Mainland," I pushed out.

Taryn gritted out, "He's too heavy and I fear they'll spot us—"

Kalen's jaw dropped. "That was you two?" He slid under my arm to hold me up instead of my wee lass.

"Later," I forced out. "No time."

Taryn eyed Kalen. "You can carry him to the ferry?"

"Aye, Black Beak. I know a witch on the mainland too."

Taryn lowered her voice. "The carrion will come after me and Finn."

Kalen replied with a curt nod and turned to me. "Come on, mate." Repositioning himself under my arm, he encouraged me to jump onto his back. Once my legs were secure beneath his arms, he sprinted toward the docks, Taryn at his side. The jolting motion ripped fresh pain through me. I wanted to black out and feel nothing. But not while Taryn was in danger. Not while we still couldn't be more than fifteen feet apart.

But it was useless.

I was growing too listless from the enormity of pain.

The last thing I remembered was Taryn cradling me to her on

the ferry. Her fingers running through the dark green hair falling around my face. Her lips pressed to my temple, her choked, tear-stained pleas begging for me to stay with her.

"Find happiness . . ." I whispered as the world around me faded to black.

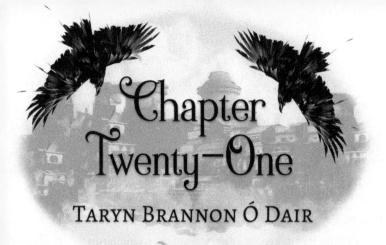

Chapter Twenty-One

TARYN BRANNON Ó DAIR

Abird swooped from a tree branch and I flinched. Every bird every caw, any shadow that moved spurred my heart into a panic. It was only a matter of time before Ren or another found us. Escaping to the mainland was almost too easy with the crowds as our shields and the fire as our distraction. But Corvus Rook knew we were on his roof and that we had disappeared into his attic. And he knew why.

Kalen swept an assessing gaze over the woods through ruffled midnight strands. His dark blue eyes unnerved me, always had. Unlike Finn's, his fae eyes were more creature than not—sharp, appearing reptilian at times. Especially now as he remained on alert.

For nearly two hours, we had traveled toward a witch Kalen claimed would bargain fairly with us. One who lived outside of a village in Caledona Wood. The poor male had carried Finn over his shoulder without complaint. Exhaustion dragged our steps. Hunger gnawed on our stomachs. A persistent headache swelled just behind my eyes, from crying, from the smoke. From the acute fear of losing Finn and the acute fear that Corvus, Rook, or Ren would find me.

Leaves crunched beneath our boots. The loud roar of wind rustling the leaves moved above us. Behind the sounds of trees, however, the trickling babble of water caught my ear. Kalen heard it too and gestured with his head to follow. He moved off trail to a stream and gently laid Finn onto the mossy ground.

Falling to my knees, I cupped water to my mouth first, drinking until my stomach felt fuller, then filled my canteen. Finn groaned. The first sound he had made in hours. I twisted where I knelt and gasped.

Kalen had lifted Finn's shirt. Rot purpled the skin fringing his wound, almost like a bruise but with a graying look of decay. Tiny black lines of poison stretched up his chest and across his stomach like roots. Bile coated my throat and I started to gag as fresh tears sprang to my eyes. I didn't think I was capable of more tears.

Who had cursed him?

A faint memory of the hag at the ball came to mind. Had she cursed Finn for stealing the amulet? It was the only logical answer. And he didn't tell me. I was so pissed at him and his no pity-fussing rule. Pissed and terrified.

My gaze darted around for something I could wildcraft to draw out the infection. I should have thought of this sooner. But I could think of nothing else but finding the Sisters Three or Kalen's witch. Over my shoulder, I spotted rib wort, a variety of common plantain, and a surge of relief rolled through me. I plunked my canteen into my pack before gathering several broad leaves for now and several more for later. At the stream bank, I grabbed two rocks to use as a pestle and mortar, quickly pulverizing the leaves to release their medicinal properties.

Quickly but gently, I began packing the infected wound with the bruised rib wort. Finn sucked air in through clenched teeth, his face pinched in a grimace. But he didn't wake. I rummaged through my pack for strips of Finn's old shirt to wrap around his side, loosening a tight breath when my fingers closed around the scrap linen.

Kalen watched me closely. "You know the healing arts."

"My parents own an apothecary on Seren."

His brows pushed together. "The Kettle's Thyme? Explains your finer dialect."

I sighed. "Black Beak changed my last name after my parents legally disowned me. The only part of my life I didn't mind them stealing."

Kalen nodded. It was common enough to be renamed in the guilds. Turning toward the stream, he cupped water into his hands, brought it close to his mouth, and began whispering words in a language I didn't know. A glimmer of sparkling light snaked across the surface. He had elemental magic? Slowly, he trickled the enchanted water over Finn's wound.

"Water has healing properties too," Kalen murmured. "Not enough to reverse this curse, mind you. But the arsehole might return to consciousness."

"Lift him a little." Kalen slowly angled Finn upward and I made quick work bandaging up his wound. Pointing to the shimmering water droplets, I said, "I've only seen Finn use coercion magic."

"He lost connection to his earth magic years ago, lass." Kalen lowered Finn back to the moss, then met my eyes. "I wasn't a wee one like Finn when soldiers marched into my corner of The Wilds . . ."

Kalen's words trailed off, his dark brows forming a scowl. He lifted his pierced ear toward the tree canopy just as the forest around us grew strangely quiet. An unnatural stillness that lifted the hairs on the back of my neck. His eyes snapped above my head.

"We have incoming company," he whispered in a low, warning growl.

The sky darkened above us almost immediately. The blood drained from my head and pooled into my already nauseated gut. Ravens. Their caws thundered and screeched through the stillness of the forest. How had we not heard them approach until now?

Memories flooded my mind of beaks and talons in my hair, birds attacking my arms, my back. I had to keep myself from running. The damn curse would force me and Finn to collide if I did.

While my panicking pulse watched the sky, a raven swooped down and materialized before smoothly landing on the ground.

Materialized into a male with feathery black hair that fell over dark purple eyes.

Holy mother of stars. I grabbed my pack and jumped to my feet. I knew I would see him eventually. But I wasn't prepared for the sight of him arriving as a raven and shifting before my eyes.

"Hello, pet." Ren stepped toward me in an impeccable black

suit, his black wings dragging behind him. Ones he explicitly wanted me to now see. But I wasn't that fifteen-year-old girl who swooned at a boy's dangerous beauty anymore. Especially his. Arching a brow, I tightened my expression and a corner of his mouth ticked up in a dark smile. "There's the *fire* I remember," he purred, each word dripping with derision. "One I *clearly* under-estimated."

Kalen sidled up beside me and flashed his small canines, a pocketknife in his grip.

"Are you the son of Corvus or Rook, Ren Cormac?" I de-manded.

Ren cocked his head, eerily similar to a bird. How did I not see it before? "Dearest Taryn," he said in that slithering melodi-ous voice of his, "I *am* the Corvus Rook."

My heart dropped to my stomach. He was *what?!*

Corvus Rook was a title?

He played the guilds against each other too?

A wicked smile shadowed Ren's illusion of charm. He took a slow step toward me. "All of Seren is mine." Another sensual step closer. "I'm *the king* of the carrion crime syndicate. And you," he snarled, "set fire to *my* kingdom."

I instinctually took a step back.

Kalen grabbed my arm and positioned himself in front of me. "Finn," I whispered urgently to him. Understanding my warn-ing, he glanced at the ravens and swore under his breath. Turn-ing, he bumped into me, using the motion to slide his pocketknife into my fingers. A weapon I quickly hid behind the pack strapped across my shoulder.

My gaze swiveled back to Ren, who slowed just before me. That bastard had sold and purchased innocent lives. Our tears, our pain were his gain. I didn't know how old he really was or how many other girls he had tricked.

But he would *not* steal another's freedom again.

"It takes a special kind of perverted pleasure," I gritted out, "to have all that power and still lower yourself to trick common girls into indentured slavery."

Delight danced in his soulless gaze. "Give me the Eye of Lugh and Amulet of Oisín, stupid mortal." His soft, lyrical tone washed over me. I could feel the ripple of magic in each word.

Why didn't he just use physical force to steal the Eye back? Was there something weird about its magic? Probably. Or did he just want to mess with my head?

I was so over faerie riddles and laws and bargains.

Even though I was pissed, my legs were shaking—to dash into the woods, to fall to the ground and curl into a fetal position. Phantom talons tangled in my hair and the ghostly feel of sharp beaks pecked at my arms. Still, I flashed Ren a taunting grin and snapped, "Go choke on worm-ridden shite, you disgusting chicken!"

The intensity of Ren's stare darkened to a starless indigo sky, a gaze that drifted toward the cloud of ravens. His mouth parted, one I used to dream about endlessly kissing, and words in an unfamiliar lilting language fell into the air. The hairs on my arms stood on end. How was he still commanding ravens? I had the Eye of Lugh in my possession. I couldn't tell if these birds had tags or not either.

Gripping the knife tighter, I studied the angle of his neck.

The ravens cawed, a flocked war cry, and dove toward where I stood.

"Taryn Hunt," Ren tried again, my name melodious and drenched in magic—

The muscles in my shoulders bunched. My legs locked in for balance.

"—*Give me* the Eye of Lugh and Amulet of Oisín."

Pushing out a hot, furious breath, I swung my arm, the knife aimed at his jugular. A beautifully cruel curl of his lip was all I saw before he shifted into a raven. The point of the small blade sliced through air. I turned in place, my gaze frantically darting around. My breath came quick, hard.

"Do you know why I cased you, pet?" his voice sang from behind me. I spun to a raven in a low branch just as the writhing warband of birds descended.

"Taryn!" Kalen shouted.

The heavy beat of wings rushed in my ears. Talons sank into my shoulder. Beaks pecked at my legs, back, torso. I screamed, blocking the attacking birds with my arms. Kalen threw himself over Finn and covered both of their heads with his hands.

Ren materialized back into his fae form before me. "Alcoholic father. Bitter, vain mother. You were so desperate to fly the nest, it was easy to trick you into the mortal construct of a faerie tale happy ending." Contempt lined his lips. "Easy to trick, but I only case the girls who will be the hardest to break."

He morphed into his raven form and I lost him in the storm of wings and talons.

Lifting the knife, I tried to pivot on my heel. But the birds continued to relentlessly attack me.

"Taryn," he sang into my ear and I jumped. "I do *not* go to the mainland. But I trust no other to retrieve the Eye of Lugh. For this and for Seren, I will *personally* break you until *nothing* of you remains but a hollow husk for my pleasure."

The ravens parted for him and I folded into myself, every part of me trembling—with fear, with rage. Baring my teeth in a guttural scream, I charged with the knife. Once more, he shifted into a raven and flew out of reach. Breath heaved from my burning lungs in large gulps. I shot a glance at Finn who remained unconscious. Kalen continued to hover over him, his eyes wide and haunted.

Where was the Maiden? These were *her* requested objects. After sending ravens to aid us, I would think she would be a bit more invested now that we were on the mainland.

My mind skidded to a stop. *Maiden. Ravens.*

The most important part of the legend, Taryn, wasn't that she was a virgin. Any maid would do, if so.

Finn's voice soothed my terrified soul.

It was that she be beautiful. And, love, your beauty is now proven legendary.

I knew then as I did now that he wasn't complimenting me just on my physical looks. I had held rare power over a faerie monster. So rare, it apparently belonged to legend.

Ren appeared before me once more, a daggered edge to his arrogant smile. Ravens dipped and dove at me. Hot tears limned my eyes and I pushed back the bile creeping up my throat. He would *not* break me. I would set all Seren on fire, not just his casi-no, before he could own one more piece of me. Or clip the wings of another for his amusement and profit.

My fingers tremored, but I reached into my pack and pulled out the Eye of Lugh. Ren locked onto the orb—no longer illu-sioned as a planter and fern—and his entire body went unnat-urally still. His gaze, however, bordered on unhinged. I didn't know what to do. If I could disable one monster, however, maybe I could disable another. I had to try.

Ren's hand struck out to grab the Eye from my palm. The ra-vens around me circled faster.

"Land," I commanded into the orb. "You are no longer bound to the Raven Folk, Ren Cormac." The Eye flashed a purple light. I sucked in a sharp gasp. It responded to me? Shock registered on Ren's darkly handsome face, too. The wide-eyed look of surprise grimacing into a scowl when the coerced birds swooped to the ground and faced me.

Twinkling shite on a cracker!

Friends, I commanded an army of ravens. *An. Army. Of. Ra-vens.*

Kalen gaped at me as he eased up from Finn.

I lifted the orb to my mouth again, ready to command the birds to attack the faerie who had stolen our lives, our freedoms. The true thief among us. But I also didn't want to force the old fae to do anything that may be against their will. For now, they were peaceful.

But maybe the Eye could speak to the Maiden, who also com-manded ravens.

"Sisters Three," I spoke to the orb, "I have all three objects requested. Find me." The purple light flashed once more and I grinned.

Ren's mouth twisted in fury, his eyes black fire. He reached for me just as a different conspiracy of ravens darkened the sky. The thunder of their caws rolled through the forest. Panic slackened Ren's jaw. He jumped back a step, his black wings outstretched. The male peered at me, then the surrounding woods, a spooked glint in his rounded eyes.

Did he know the Sisters Three? The skunk ornaments had his knees knocking too, did they?

I almost started laughing—but a groan reached my ears. *Finn!*

Clutching the orb and knife to my chest, I whipped my head over my shoulder in his direction.

Pale green eyes fluttered open. "Taryn," he murmured, his voice strained and breathy. "Where's my wife?" he asked Kalen.

"Kicking a Raven Folk's arse at his own game, she is." Kalen's gaze flicked to mine for half a second. The healing water was working.

A tiny smile fluttered across Finn's lips. "Tell me she has murder eyes, mate."

I didn't hear Kalen's answer.

A cottage landed into sudden existence, barely a rustle in the leaves at its arrival. Smoke curled from the chimney, a homey look as if the Crone had lived on the edge of the stream for an age. The same stars damned smoke that taunted me eight days ago.

Ren fluttered his wings, lifting into the air. "I will find you, pet—"

"Pet," a raspy voice said at my side and Ren froze in the air.

"Shite!" I hissed, my heart now beating outside of my body. How in the dark moons had the Crone reached my side so fast? I nearly rolled my eyes at myself. The witch traveled by cottage through the woods and I was mystified by how she appeared at my side without my knowing?

"Pretty blackbird," the Crone said. "We finally drew you away from your nest in the sky."

My mouth fell open.

Was she suggesting this was all a ruse to get Ren to the mainland?

Ren couldn't speak or move, I realized. He was in a paralyzed state, the same one Finn and I had experienced right before we were cursed.

"Fifty years, Corvus Rook, you have owned what does not belong to you," the Crone said. "Fifty years, Ren Cormac, you shall now spend as my *pet for stealing the Eye of Lugh from my personal possession.*" The Crone turned her milky eyes my way. "The objects, Taryn Hunt of Beggar's Hole."

I swallowed thickly. Every part of me ached to look at Finn one last time before our mate bond was severed. If I did, though, I would beg to remain cursed at his side until my dying breath. Closing my eyes in a long, pained blink, I pushed back the rising grief and reached into my bag for the tooth and amulet.

"Maiden," Finn called out and my heart didn't know if it wanted to soar above the stars in hope or drown in my building sorrow. "I want to bargain."

My eyes shot to his over my shoulder and he winked.

Chapter Twenty-Two

FINN BRANNON Ó DAIR

Kalen helped me sit up. Bargaining from my back like an invalid was not how I wanted to be remembered in the stories told to the generations to come of how a virile, devilishly handsome fae male and a legendary mortal beauty cunningly defeated the carrion foes of Seren. My kind were formed from the magic and strength of oaks. I could weather a variety of tribulations.

But not on my back like an old, sick ancient while being fussed over by my best mate.

A sharp pain knifed my side. I grimaced, then blew out a slow breath.

My gaze drifted back to my wife and my eyes finally focused. Scratches and cuts from raven talons and beaks bled in parts. Strands of hair were torn from her corded braid and fell around her face and shoulders in a wild mess. A deep growl left my chest. My fingers dug into the moss, my shaking muscles flexed. If I were not so weak, I would rip this world apart within my next breath, starting with *him*.

But that could still be arranged. I wasn't dead yet.

"What do you want from the Maiden, Finnan Ó Brannan of Primry Green?" the Crone asked me.

I thickened my accent in the way of The Wilds and Caravan fae. "I will speak to the Maiden in her form, Crone." To Taryn I said, "Hand her the Amulet of Oisín, but nothing else."

Taryn's brows wrinkled but she did as asked. The Crone caressed the ruby inlaid necklace. Then, with bony fingers, she excitedly clasped the amulet behind her neck and light exploded around her. Patchy, frizzy white hair grew out to long, silky auburn locks, a crown of flowers upon her brow. Wrinkled skin mottled with age spots smoothed to a fair, creamy complexion. Emerald green eyes shone instead of the milky white of before.

"Feck. Me," Kalen whispered beside me.

The Maiden was every lad's dream, down to the tempting curves of her body.

But her beauty paled in comparison to Taryn's. How I wanted to unbraid my wife's dark locks and feel the strands fall across my face. The lass, noting my heated stare, arched a brow at me and I replied with a flirty smirk. She started to roll her eyes, but movement in the forest caught her gaze.

The area around the Maiden's cottage cleared and a garden, brimming with flowers, herbs, and food, appeared. Gone were the overgrown brambles belonging to the Crone. Taryn gasped in delight. I knew what she was thinking. *Aye, a patch of lawn for a garden and children, just like you want, love.* To have children with

Taryn . . . sweet Dobhar-chú tears, the bairns would be absolutely feral. Just like their mother.

"You have a request of me, Fair One of the Oak?" the Maiden asked, moving toward me. Kalen straightened and cleared his throat when she knelt at my side. The dark green gown hugging her figure pooled around her feet.

"I ask for healing," I answered. "And to avenge my mate."

"And what do you offer for healing?" She tilted her head and long, auburn locks fell down her arm.

"Service to you—"

Taryn's eyes widened. "Finn, no!"

"To heal Taryn first, then me, I offer you service for three years and one day," I repeated. "Dissolve my bond with Corbie and I will fetch you magical artifacts and rare ingredients instead. But," I said, drawing the word out, "you'll provide a place for me and my mate. She will train in healing magic under you as a green witch, unbound to you." This was more than fair for three years of my life. Healing me and Taryn was basic magic for a witch like the Sisters Three. And I knew the Maiden, who embodied new beginnings, would desire to tip the scales of fate for a love story forged in renewal. But she was still fae, so I added, "You will not trick us. After three years and one day, we are free of slavery and servitude. Our lives will be our own. And, as your servant and apprentice, you will protect us."

"And for your vengeance?"

Tears streamed down Taryn's cheeks. The nicks, blood, and fraying hair destroyed me. I couldn't protect her against that Raven Folk monster and she suffered for my curse.

"To avenge my mate," I growled, "I demand Ren Cormac's life. And I will give you my coercion magic in exchange for letting me spill his blood." I held her green eyes, ones that were several shades darker than mine. "Bottle up the essence for a rainy day, Maiden. Release the persuasive whispers to a gust of wind. Bury the magic's roots back into the earth." Her eyes brightened. "Grow a Truth Telling Tree and absorb the confessions and vows of those passing by."

She wove her fingers with mine and caressed the back of my hand with her thumb. "I will heal both you and your mate for three years and one day of your service, Fair One of the Oak. The Mother says you are a seed adrift, tree spirit, and desire to set down roots and grow a family, aye?"

Warmth filled my chest and I nodded, too afraid to speak. To have a family and home I could call my own was my greatest desire.

"I agree to take your mate on as my green witch apprentice," the Maiden continued, "and will provide for your needs until your service of three years and one day is complete. Nor will we riddle you and your mate again."

My body relaxed. I could almost weep.

"Vengeance belongs to my sister Crone. Only she can truly grant your request." The Maiden turned my palm up and traced the lines of my hand. "The Mother has another message for you, though. 'By giving your mate a future, you have avenged her past.'"

"I hear the truth in the Mother's words," I said, then gritted out, "But blood for blood."

"The Crone has a message for you," she said, her mouth

tipping into a frown. "'The Corvus Rook's fate is bound to my blood oath of vengeance for fifty years before yours. The cost to avenge your mate is fifty years of revenge thirst that will not be sated until the fifty-first year."

I swallowed back another spear of pain. A flush dewed my forehead in clammy sweat. "What is your message, then, Maiden?"

Her eyes flicked to mine. "I am the spring, the renewal of life. I am the gentleness of a first kiss and the violence of falling in love."

A smile trembled across my lips. "Then I accept your offer of violence, Maiden, and the Mother's wisdom in reaping a harvest many years sown. The Crone can have her vengeance."

"And your coercion magic?" the Maiden asked me.

My smile widened. "We have three years and one day to bargain, aye?"

"Very well, Fair One of the Oak."

"I do have one request for you without condition," I rushed out. The Maiden tipped her head to continue. "I ask the Crone to lend Taryn her magic to turn that bastard tail feather into a skunk. Fair payment for the harm and torment you put my mate through to aid your sister's vengeance."

"You love the mortal truly."

"Aye, Maiden," I answered her softly but my eyes were fastened to Taryn's. "I would sacrifice all for her happiness."

"Yes," she said simply. "I saw so in my scrying bowl and that's why I sent a bird to tempt Corvus Rook into stealing my weather ring. It was not only a gift for sister Crone. Your future love stirred my magic then as it does now. The love of True Mates forged through a curse and tethered in the breaking. It is a gift from the gods. Training in fae magic under me will gift her a life as long as the elves, too."

I sucked in a shocked breath. Taryn would live as long as me? I didn't know wielding fae magic would affect a mortal so. I only wanted my wife to have her dream. My gaze drifted over to Taryn, my True Mate, and stars . . . the most beautiful smile blushed across her lips and my heart leapt from my chest to bow at her feet.

"The Crone and I will grant you this request without condition." The Maiden released my hand and stood to approach Taryn. My mate stared at the Sisters Three wide-eyed. "Greetings, new witchling," the Maiden said as she healed Taryn's wounds. When finished, she leaned in and whispered in Taryn's ear, then took her hand to impart magic.

My wee beam of unicorn sunshine turned the full force of her dark, wild storm onto the piece of shite still hovering in the air. I could see all the words she wanted to say in her thundering eyes, all the words she didn't know how to say too. He wasn't worth more of her time, though. Taryn seemed to come to this conclusion as well. My lass opened her mouth and the spell the Maiden whispered into her ear rippled in the air around us.

Ren's face tightened with fury for only a blink of a second. In the next, the male poofed into a raven, still mid-flight. A second heartbeat later, he dropped to the ground as a taxidermized skunk in an expensive three-piece suit, his striped head topped with a mop of feathery black hair.

The Maiden dropped Taryn's hand to scoop up Ren the Skunk. She pet the lad's head a moment then threw him up into the air where he disappeared. "He's in sister Crone's storage now."

A cawed cry filled the sky, a celebratory song the grounded ravens echoed. Taryn tilted her head back to watch the aerial dance. Beside her, the Maiden lifted her hands to the setting sun and sang in Raven tongue, as Ren had, and—

Taryn sucked in a sharp breath and stiffened.

What in the seven moons?!

I did not see this coming. Though perhaps I should have.

Now standing before us were the ravens Taryn coerced to land—fully shifted into their fae form while joining the Maiden in song, a beautiful lilting sound of freedom. In the sky, half of the birds swooped to the ground and shifted beside the other Raven Folk. The remaining half—old fae—continued to dance beneath the first glimmer of starlight.

"Taryn Hunt." A Raven Folk—in a dark red gown hemmed in black feathers and a shiny black top hat tilted on her head— slowed before my mate. "I am Ravenna, but you know me as S725."

Taryn blinked back her surprise. "He enslaved his own Folk?"

"Ren Cormac stole my crown and title and bound us Folk to him before Seren existed, witchling. He bound the wood ravens to him with the Eye of Lugh afterward. The Maiden, however, freed me and a few others years ago in a bargain to spy for her."

"You heard my agreement with the tree spirit?" the Maiden

asked Ravenna.

"Aye," Ravenna replied. "And the other?"

The Maiden answered in Raven while walking toward me, but it was too quiet to make out.

"As you say," Ravenna replied in Carran's common tongue

"What will happen to Seren?" Kalen asked beside me.

Ravenna's lips quirked into a smile. "I am the new Corvus Rook, Kalen Kelly. The rightful queen of my Folk. Seren is now *my* nest." Ravenna's gaze slid to mine next and she dipped her head. "Finnan Ó Brannon of The Wilds and Traveler Folk, per the Maiden's agreement, your debts are cleared. You are bound to Seren's Ravens no more."

"And also per our agreement," the Maiden added, touching my head, "you are healed."

A tingling warmed my wrist. The Thieves' Guild mark faded and I choked back a sob. That same moment, iron shackles on my spirit fell away and the earth rushed up to thrum in my veins and pulse in tandem with my heart. Wind, infused with the happy sighs of all living greens of the forest, filled my lungs and blew away the rot of the hag's curse. I started laughing. Above me, the stars twinkled their delight at my magic's return.

"Kalen Kelly of The Wilds and Traveler Folk," Ravenna spoke next, "your debts are cleared, too, as gratitude from the Maiden for protecting Finn Brannon. You are bound to Seren's Ravens no more."

My best mate's hair floated around him, as if he were under water. The dark blues of his eyes brightened in the twilight. He lifted his hands and water droplets danced atop his fingertips.

Seren Raven Folk

We grinned at each other like absolute fools.

But there was another I wanted to share this joy with more.

Jumping to my feet, I strode toward Taryn, my smile as large as hers. Before she could speak, I cupped her face and whispered against her lips, "I promised you that I would claim what I wanted when I was free of Corbie." I caressed her bottom lip with the pad of my thumb. "You are all I want, Taryn Brannon Ó Dair." A tear-choked laugh fluttered across my skin and I fell through an endless starry night at the happy sound. A fall I never wanted to land. She was mine. All mine. "Nine hundred and ninety-three, love."

Then my heart and soul kissed hers.

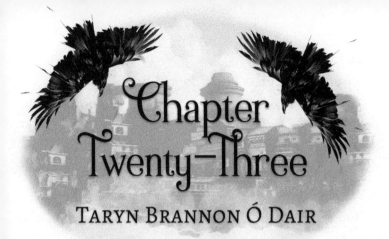

Chapter Twenty-Three

TARYN BRANNON Ó DAIR

In less than an hour, my entire life had changed. The lives of others too. My rapidly spinning emotions didn't know where to settle.

Except this . . .

Finn's lips on mine. I could drown in these sensations and never want to draw breath again. The people around us, the forest, the items still in my pack no longer mattered. Only him.

From the time I was old enough to understand romance, I believed that falling in love took months, years. But now I believed in the faerie tales. Two souls could collide under the right circumstances and feel whole for the first time. Two hearts could intertwine so fast, the beat of one craved the other to an obsession. And oh how I craved Finn Brannon.

"Lovers," the Maiden said, "we still have your curse to settle, aye?"

I pulled back and Finn smiled against my lips. "Can I give her the remaining items now?"

"Need a sixteen-foot break, do you?"

I snorted. "Your self-love will keep you company if you get lonely."

"Right now, Rynnie, I want no distance between us."

Heat spilled into my pulse. "Then you better be good. No more hiding wounds from me, Ó Dair."

"Oh I'm good, love," he quickly replied with a wink, then stepped away.

Friends, I didn't know if I wanted to punch him in the now healed wound as a reminder of the grief he put me though or kiss him until I forgot my own name. I settled for a mock disgruntled sigh instead. Then turned toward the Maiden.

Reaching into my bag, I pulled out the Dobhar-chú tooth and placed it in the Maiden's palm, who dipped her head at me.

"From the mud and clay," she intoned, "you formed your first dreams as mates, of a house, a garden, and children." The Maiden made a stitching motion over the tooth. A leather cord began to appear, wrapping itself around the edges of the tooth, the cord's ends eventually knotting together. She presented the necklace to Finn who pulled it over his neck with a crooked smile. "You both survived monsters and monstrous situations alone until the Dobhar-chú." She touched the tooth resting on Finn's chest. "You no longer fight alone."

That was . . . actually rather poetic.

Both the Maiden and Finn turned to me.

The Eye of Lugh seemed to grow heavier in my hands. Handing this over felt like handing over all the power we both fought to gain over our lives. "What will you use the Eye for?"

"To do what should have been done hundreds of suns and moons ago, witchling."

I gnawed the inside of my lip. "I could steal the Eye but the Eye has yet to be stolen from my hands. There are more of you than me. Why all this bargaining?"

"Aye," the Maiden said. "The magic is stronger when not held and half as strong when it is. To steal the Eye of Lugh while held, halves the half eternally for the thief. To gift the Eye of Lugh while held increases its holding power by half of its half."

I blinked.

Stars above, how faeries understood each other was a mystery I wasn't sure even they understood. Well, it was unrealistic to live an entire life cursed as we were. Unrealistic and dangerous. So I handed her the Eye of Lugh, granting her half of its half, whatever that meant.

The Maiden turned toward the Raven Folk and the wood ravens still flying in the moonlit night sky. "The Crone declares that you will be bound by Lugh's cursed ravens nevermore."

The orb fell from her fingers and shattered on a rock at her feet. Purple light burst out in all directions. I brought my hands up to my eyes to block the flash. The light faded into misty sparkles and two large ravens appeared. With a loud, echoing caw, they stretched out their wings and alighted into the air. Swirling around me and Finn, they released one more caw before flying toward the moon.

The Maiden announced to all, "Lugh's ravens are now free to join him in Tír na nÓg."

Ravenna held my gaze for a long beat. Then she and her fellow Folk shifted into their bird forms and departed for Seren.

"Witchling," the Maiden said to me. "You will begin your apprenticeship in fifteen days." She bowed her head at us then disappeared into the shadows.

Fifteen days? My eyes fell to my wrist and . . . a deep ache stole my breath. My skin was bare, not a hint of a single raven. Finn peered at his bare wrist too. Two heartbeats later, however, a raven reappeared on his wrist, one for his bind of servitude to the Maiden. And he smiled.

"Finn, lad," Kalen said at his side. "I'm off to Den Merrow for the night, maybe two."

"Do not leave the village without saying goodbye, mate."

"Aye, you're stuck with my fine arse." Kalen grinned at Finn, who pulled him into an embrace.

"So fine," Finn murmured humorously.

Pulling away, Kalen tipped his head at me and then wandered off into the trees.

For a few seconds, we let the night wrap around us. A light breeze fluttered the strands of dark green hair falling over one of Finn's eyes and I almost audibly sighed. The girls who fell at his feet annoyed me *before* he was mine. But now? They would feel the full force of my murderous gaze if they so much as batted an eyelash in his direction.

I shook my head. "I . . . I can't believe you indentured yourself to the Maiden for me. You could have bargained to be free."

A side of his mouth hooked up in a soft smile. "You are an official green witch herbal healer now, to be trained in magic by the Maiden herself. In Caledona Wood, that makes you legendary, lass." His smile grew rascally. "Had to ensure you kept that faerie tale status."

"Why would I lose—" I cut myself off and shot him a dry look. "You were thinking about *that* while dying and bargaining?"

Finn cupped my face and lowered his mouth until his lips barely hovered over mine. "So, Rynnie love," he crooned. "You're a virgin?"

I rolled my eyes. "Maybe I should remain a maid like my mentor. Hold two legendary tales among the fae."

"No," he said, his tone serious. "Only one tale allowed per mortal."

His lips brushed mine in a sweet, teasing kiss.

I pushed him away. "Is that actually true?"

Finn laughed and playfully pulled me back, wrapping his arms around my waist to lock me in while burying his face in my neck. I squealed in surprise and he laughed again. While smiling against my skin, Finn pressed a soft kiss to my throat where my pulse trilled.

"You own my heart," he whispered. My breath fluttered as his lips trailed up my neck. "Protecting you, caring for you," he confessed into my ear, "is the purest magic I know, Taryn."

My strong, sturdy oak. Who never hesitated to protect me from monsters or shelter me from storms. Who provided for my needs before his own, even while he was dying. Even when I didn't trust his actions to be real. This was his very nature, the root of his magic. One denied him since childhood.

My heart . . . it was breaking in the most exquisite way.

He was so infuriatingly beautiful.

And all mine.

The tips of my fingers traced the lines of his jaw, his bottom lip. "I have a bargain for you, Finn Brannon." I trailed the same fingers along his ear, to the point. He quietly moaned as his entire body shivered; his eyes closed in a long, languid blink. "Set down roots with me and I will be your home."

"Rynnie . . ." he murmured on a shaky breath.

"Grow a family with me, Finnan, and I will grant you one real swoon per week."

His mouth slanted in a mischievous flirty look that was all Finn. "Two real swoons and three stolen kisses."

"Two stolen kisses and one not-a-surprise-attack kiss."

"Only one non-stolen kiss?" Finn huffed a disbelieving laugh. "No deal, love."

I arched a brow. "What's your counter bargain, then."

"To grow a family with you, my wee feisty otter wife," he said, resting his hands on my hips. "Be mine in this lifetime and in the world beyond." He paused a dramatic beat. "And seven real swoons per week. Once per day, minimum."

I stepped out of his embrace with a mock impatient look. "Go on then. Better start making me swoon before I change my mind."

And, just like at the mineral spring, his humor quickly faded into a molten look that heated my already flushing skin. Those pale green eyes lingered on my mouth a heady beat, a small canine biting down on the corner of his bottom lip. Sweet moons above, just that look alone made me lightheaded. In a single, sultry blink, his hungry gaze flicked to mine as he gripped the hem of his shirt and started lifting the garment over his head, inch by maddening inch, tossing it to the mossy ground.

Muscles danced across his chest and shoulders with the motion. The hard ridges of his abdomen flexed as his arms lowered and I was on the verge of panting. My fingers grazed his unmarred side where the wound was only minutes earlier. I wanted to taste his skin, to know every contoured line of his body. My fingers trailed down the defined V of his lower hip and hooked onto the hem of his pants. Falling stars, he was beautiful in ways poets could never capture.

Finn played with the tip of my braid, then tugged on the ribbon and affectionately began unplaiting my hair. "I, Finnan Brannon Ó Dair, mate bind myself to you, Taryn Brannon Ó Dair, for as long as our souls exist." His lips were a butterfly wing caress across mine. A fragile touch, as if this feeling might shatter at any moment. I feared this were all a dream too. Sinking his fingers into the dark tresses falling loose around my waist, he cradled my face and whispered, "I am entirely yours, wife, for now and for all eternity."

His mouth softly claimed mine. I melted into the tender press of his lips, the slow branding sweep of his tongue an owning I felt in the marrow of my soul.

We were free of Seren.

Free of our curse.

Tilting my head up, he leaned in to deepen our kiss.

And our bodies exploded into motion.

Electricity crackled in every contact. Each touch was desperate, frantic. Our chests heaving. We couldn't pull the other in close enough. After fighting for this moment, separation, of any kind, was unthinkable.

Back in the warehouse, I had ached to be his with every breath in my body. Any future without Finn at my side was unimaginable. But to feel this pleasure, to possess his affection before he was free of Seren would have obliterated my heart in a slow, agonizing death.

Now I wanted to be destroyed by him.

My hands roamed the warm, smooth skin of his chest, across his broad shoulders, down the defined muscles of his arms. The arms that protected me since our first day cursed. I would never tire of touching him, of loving him. My fingers trailed lower and lower to the belt on his waist and his breath trembled.

He grabbed my wrist and softly tugged me to the ground as he fell to his knees. His lips left mine to kiss down my neck. Gently, he uncurled his fingers from my hand and unbuckled my belt, letting it fall to the ground. Without missing a beat, he gripped the hem of my shirt and pulled it over my head.

My first instinct was to cover up, but his bewitched gaze held me captive.

"Beautiful," he breathed. At the rough sound of his voice, moonlight spilled into my veins and pooled low in my belly. "Taryn—"

"Don't you dare stop."

With a sensual curve to his smile, he lowered me beneath him and whispered, "Seduce me with dangerous words like that and you might riddle us both—"

I grabbed his face and tasted his swollen lips once more. At this moment, I didn't care what I riddled him into as long I could feel his quickening pulse burning beside mine.

Finn moaned into our kiss. A deep, low growl. My entire being vibrated at the possessive sound. His fingers traced the curve of my bare breast and I lost myself to his searing touch. His demanding lips. The completeness of his breath tangling with mine.

Still, we needed more. Needed to be closer.

He quickly peeled away the rest of my clothing, then removed his. Flashing me a devilish smile, Finn pressed his lips to my calf, my thigh, moving higher and . . . *sweet gods*. Starlight burst inside me. I became pure sensation, bright and all-consuming. I sank into the moss, my fingers gripping in his hair. A moan left me, his name a plea. I clutched at the strands tighter as curling heat began building, building. Before I came apart, he lightly kissed my stomach, a wicked curve to his mouth.

Tantalizing warmth shivered across my skin.

This was absolute torture.

Eyes locked onto mine, he slowly made his way up my body and dark skies, I was mesmerized by the graceful, sensual display of muscle. His masculine beauty, especially here, among the trees, set fire to a hundred blazing suns in my fevering blood.

If he didn't make me his in every sense soon, I was pretty sure I would perish—and he knew it.

A flirty smile teased his lips as he settled above me.

I would roll my eyes at his cocksure arrogance. But I was too worked up. Instead, I pulled on the string tying his hair up and sighed as the disheveled tresses fell to his shoulders.

"Swooning yet, love?"

"No," I lied with a pointed arch of my brow. "Not even close."

Finn lifted my leg to hook over his hip. The satisfied slant of his lips softened into a look so sinful, I would agree to any bargain he made right now. Hell, I might bargain just for him to hurry up before I went mad. The male knew exactly what he was doing to me, too. That sensual grin widened as he lowered onto his forearm and adjusted his position. Silky, dark green strands curtained around our faces, his lips close to mine.

And in one shared breath the energy between us tilted.

Flirtations and teasing shifted to the loud pounding of our hearts.

"Taryn . . ." The tenderness in how he whispered my name spilled drowsy bliss into the dizzy sensations already spinning through me. His nose brushed along my jaw and my eyes fluttered closed. "My love."

"I'm yours," I whispered back. "All of me."

Finn captured my lips in a bruising kiss. His muscles moved beneath my hands. I gripped his hip and, gently, reverently, he pushed in until nothing separated us. No rival guilds. No corrupt laws. No slavers who stole children for profit.

We stilled, savoring the heady rush of completeness, our breaths heavy, our twining pulses on fire.

Then he began to move.

I exploded into a million stars.

A beautiful violence of the soul as his melded with mine.

My moans formed his name, my fingers dug into his back, needing him closer, closer, closer. At the sound of my unraveling, a soft, territorial growl left Finn's chest. I couldn't think, only feel. The deep, languid way his body moved, a slow dance of wild emotion, shattered me into reforged wholeness.

I was fervently drunk on him. Intoxicated beyond repair.

"I love you," he whispered, into my neck, into my shoulder, as he kissed along my jaw and nipped at my earlobe.

A smile feathered across my swollen lips. "I love you," I whispered back.

He dragged his mouth back to mine and the world ceased to exist. It was just us. We owned all of time, each drop of happiness, every thread of magic. Delicious heat began building in my core again—hotter and hotter until my body was begging to become embered ash in his hands.

Finn's rhythm grew more impassioned, his kiss hungrier.

A deep moan left him as his muscles tensed. At the sound of him coming undone, my heart fell through the glittering night sky beside his. And holy mother of stars, this moonlit rush. The entire heavens rippled down my body in powerful waves. I was coming apart faster than my wild pulse could follow. Tears lined my lashes. This feeling was so beautiful, my heart ached. *He* was beautiful.

His eyes held mine, our chests heaving. I cupped his face and caressed the corner of his lip with my thumb—and paused. My wrist was still bare. A quick glance at the other confirmed the same.

Biting down on my lower lip, I pushed Finn to his back and rolled atop him.

And then, with the stars and trees as my witness, I began. "I,

Taryn Brannon Ó Dair, mate bind myself to you, Finn Brannon Ó Dair, for as long as our souls exist." I brushed a lock of hair from his face and tucked it behind the point of his ear. "I belong to you, husband, for now and for all eternity."

Warmth tingled on my wrist and a smile broke out across my face.

Finn brought my new raven mark to his mouth, the tip of his tongue teasing my skin. "True Mate . . ." he whispered. Then an impish smile teased his lips and my eyes narrowed. "You waited to find out if I lived up to my earlier promise first."

"Your earlier—" I quietly groaned.

"Admit it, lass," he said, holding onto my hips. "I'm good."

"I wouldn't know," I answered with a shrug. "I've only been with the male who ruined my legendary maidenhood magic. I no longer have virgin powers because of you."

Finn grinned. "Aye, love. But my virile, irresistibly attractive magic secured you new legendary powers." He winked. "Because I'm that good."

Laughter sputtered past my attempts to appear unimpressed. "You're an eejit."

He pulled me down until our lips touched in a sweet, gentle kiss. "I love you, my wee witchling forest cat."

"I already swooned for you today, Finn."

"Once daily . . . *minimum*. That was our agreement."

Of course, it was.

"Well," I said on a weary sigh, "you'll have to work twice as hard if you want two swoons in one evening."

Finn grabbed me around the waist and flipped me beneath

him. "Deal."

"Are you serious?"

He kissed up my neck to my ear and, in a low, husky voice, whispered, "Fluffy bunny."

I burst into laughter.

Moons above, I wanted to roll my eyes so hard.

Instead, I let Finn love me again. And again. And again. Until we lay asleep in each other's arms beneath the swaying trees and twinkling stars.

Who knew that the boy who stole the ring I thieved would be the one I married—and twice.

We were partners in crime, he and I.

Attached at the hip now for an eternity.

I could think of no better happily ever after than having Finn Brannon forever at my side.

Epilogue

5 years, 4 months, 21 days later

TARYN BRANNON Ó DAIR

I stumbled over a rock and started to pitch forward. If not for Finn's firm grasp on my arm, I would probably be eating dirt. The mischievous elf had blindfolded me in the village with promises of a grand surprise. And so here I was, traipsing through the forest after a long day of filling orders to one of Finn's whims. Though, I secretly loved them.

"Almost there, Rynnie."

I huffed. "You've been saying that since we left the village."

"Well, each step forward *is* one step closer to *there*."

I quietly groaned. Faeries and their stars damned riddles.

"Da," Anlainn, our three-year-old daughter said at my side. "Almost there?"

"Aye, my wee skunklet."

"I don't stink," she protested. I could almost imagine her adorable wrinkling nose. "Brother does."

Kieran, our fifteen-month-old son, had fallen asleep on Finn's shoulder shortly after leaving the apothecary shop. His nappy, thankfully, was clean—for now.

"Remember our bargain, Annie love?" Finn asked our daughter.

"I can—" she demonstrated an excited gasp. "But no tell Mum."

"And if you keep the surprise to yourself?"

Anlainn giggled. "Da is horsey."

Finn laughed. "That was *not* our bargain, lass."

"New bargain," she said with another giggle.

I could feel Finn wobble on if he should strike a new deal with our daughter. She was a wily one, our Annie. And Finn couldn't resist her faerie child antics.

Before he could answer her, Anlainn gasped. A loud, dramatic sound. I almost laughed. She was so much like her father, it was ridiculous.

Finn pressed a kiss to my temple. "You can take the blindfold off now."

I pulled the scrap of fabric off my eyes and squinted with the sudden light. I had been blindfolded for at least thirty minutes. The landscape faded into view. My eyes caught on a small, two-story cabin with a covered porch. Rows of stone-lined garden beds filled up a large patch of lawn in the back—

A patch of lawn for a garden.

Nearby, Anlainn twirled in a field of wildflowers at the treeline, singing a song to herself. Her forest green hair flew around her as she spun round and round, her sweet, little freckled face lifted to the waning sunlight.

With enough room for a bairn or two to romp around.

My eyes lifted over the cabin's roof. In the far background, the snow-capped mountains of our neighboring kingdom peeked above a misty evening fog.

I clapped a hand over my mouth and twisted toward Finn, tears gathering on my lashes.

My strong oak, who never failed to protect and shelter his family.

A gentle breeze played with the dark green strands angled over the pale eyes locked onto mine. Our son was nuzzled into his neck, his cheeks flushed with sleep. Kieran's earthen hair curled at the ends, hiding his tiny, pointed ears.

"How?" I choked out.

Fin flashed me a pleased smile. "The Maiden."

"She gave this to us?" My face fell. "What did you agree to, Finn?"

"Calm your darling heaving bosoms," he drawled out, returning the flat look. "Nothing I hadn't already offered. The Sisters Three accepted my coercion magic for the *opportunity* and supplies to build us a home."

My mouth fell open. "You built this?"

"Aye, for four years now."

"All those jobs the Maiden gave you?—" I cut myself off and made air quotes while saying, "'Opportunities.'"

"The Maiden had many *opportunities* for me." The smug grin he shot my way was so Finn I had to roll my eyes. He stepped closer to me and lowered his voice. "And we're really only ten minutes from the shop."

The arse made me walk for thirty minutes blindfolded. I glared at him, which only made his arrogant smile widen. He was lucky he was holding our son or I would punch his arm.

Bending down, he kissed my forehead and I melted. "What do you think, my wee feisty otter wife?"

"I think I love you, Finn Brannon."

He grinned. "Come, Rynnie love."

Weaving his fingers with mine, he tugged me toward the cabin. I casually glanced over my shoulder as we walked. In the distance, Seren floated above Caledona Wood. A constant reminder of a time when we had to thieve to pay for a life stolen from us.

I peered at the cabin again just as Anlainn dashed past us, throwing flower petals into the air. Finn was not much older than her when he lost everything. My children would always know they were wanted, even when they made mistakes. And my mate? Well . . .

Mainlanders, gather around for one last lesson. Don't be afraid to let him catch your heart, even if he's an arrogant, mischievous, irritating sack of bargaining potatoes. Remind him of your everlasting devotion by promising to murder him with your pining looks. And, friends, most of all, swoon with every breath in your body. For there is nothing in this world or the next comparable to the way he'll love you.

Or the thrill of loving him back.

At the door, I turned the knob, and spun toward the faerie boy who owned my heart. "To new beginnings."

"It's not proper to seduce me in front of the children, Taryn." Lifting our hands, he kissed the raven mark on my wrist—

"Da!" Anlainn shouted from inside. "Horsey!"

I snorted a laugh.

A rascally smile flirted the corners of Finn's mouth. My only warning before he curved those very lips to mine in a slow, soft stolen kiss. "Nine-hundred and ninety-nine, love."

Then he walked past me with a wink.

Stars, how I loved his thieving ways.

The End

But also not *not* the end.

(keep flipping, you'll see what I mean)

Taryn, my sweet whiskered alley rat, the one my soul calls . . .

A small fearsome lass

Beautiful, mud-covered maid in a faerie tale

Hissing opossum

Lass

Love

Mate

Mortal

My Black Beak lass

My feisty forest cat

My feisty skunk ornament

My future skunk mate

My love

My mate who wasn't my mate but who might also be my soul-mate

My Pegasus glitter beam of sunshine

My swearing sweet potato

My sweet, naive, beautiful virgin faerie tale maid, my adorable wee otter wife

My True Mate

My wee beam of unicorn sunshine

My wee feisty otter wife

My wee feisty potato

My wee lass

My wee murderous thieving potato
My wee otter wife
My wee unicorn beam of sunshine
My wee witchling forest cat
My wee, but much, much older forest cat
My wife, my mate
Rynnie
Rynnie love
Sunshine
The tiny feisty lass
You wee thing

Taryn Brannon Ó Dair

The list of Finn's nicknames and endearments for Taryn
comprised by my #MooCrew reader, Sarah Carner.

Thank You Reader

Thank you, dear reader, for adventuring across the pages with Finn and Taryn. I will forever be your fangirl if you took a few seconds to leave a 1-2 sentence review. It doesn't have to be fancy. Just something to make the Amazon robots happy. Because when the Amazon robots are happy, I can write more books. Believe it or not, reviews keep an author in business.

Want more from the Bound by Ravens world? Of course you do!

Next up is THE NIGHT MARKET, a tale about star-crossed fated lovers Rhylen Lonan of the Caravan fae and the mortal girl with the Sight his Raven Folk tribe owns, Filena Merrick.

Also, you'll see Kalen Kelly's fine arse again in his own book that takes place in The Wilds, which may involve a bit (or a lot) of river pirating. A stowaway village girl he first flirts with at a tavern might be along for the ride too.

To get first peeks at these upcoming books, the character art, scene snippets, and more, be sure to:

1) sign up for my newsletter, MoonTree Readers

2) join my reader group, Forest Tales Readers and Moon-Tree Readers

Forest Tales Readers   MoonTree Readers

tips top hat to you

Thank You Friends

No book is complete without a team of stylists to glam it up as much as possible for ultimate reader magic. And I am lucky to have the best people in my corner to ensure my worlds, characters, and stories are the bees knees.

THE MOO CREW

Andra Prewett, Jessica Maass, Jill Bridgeman, Kelly Stepp Michelle Downing, Nicole Manus, Sarah Carner, Sarah Jordan, and Victoria Cascarelli . . . my wee feisty forest cats, thank you for alpha-ing and beta-ing for Taryn's and Finn's story. I swear on a cooked potato my endless gratitude. If you hear haunting moos in the bootlegger walls, only good luck for you! Also, one last thing . . . TARYN HUNT! *squawks*

AUTHOR BETA READERS

Robin D. Mahle, Elle Madison, and Hanna Sandvig . . . thank

you my wee otter work wives for loving on my story and cheering me on as I drafted and finalized this fae romantasy romp. Endless dobhar-chú blessings on you! I mean, they're so cute, right?

TATER MCTOT

Kelly Stepp, you are the best potato faerie assistant an author could have at her side. Thank you for always taking good care of my publishing company and author branding and stories and . . . me.

I look forward to more bookish adventures with you *high-fives in bad boys with awesome hair*

KATE ANDERSON

I adore you lady! Thanks for always lending me your eagle eye on my manuscript and sending me hilarious memes. They always make my day!

THE STARRY KINGDOMS OF
THE FAE LADIES

Angela J. Ford, Alisha Klapheke, Eliza Tilton, Jessica M. Butler, Stephanie BwaBwa, Nicole Zoltack, Nicki Chapelway, Megan Charlie, Jes Drew, and Jamie Dalton . . .Thank you for the laughs, support, and kindredness. And special thanks to Angela J. Ford and Stephanie BwaBwa for organizing this collection. You two are faetastic!

And now, I'm off to write THE NIGHT MARKET . . .

More Books

BY JESIKAH SUNDIN

THE BIODOME CHRONICLES

ECO-DYSOTOPIAN FAERIE TALE

She is locked inside an experimental world.
He has never met the girl who haunts his dreams.
A chilling secret forever binds their lives together.

 LEGACY
ELEMENTS
TRANSITIONS
GAMEMASTER

THE EALDSPELL CYCLE

EPIC FAERIE TALES WITH A HISTORICAL FANTASY TWIST

Dreams are dangerous . . .
Unless she unlocks the powers of her mind.
He fights his Otherworld shadow self.
And with only fae magic to re-spin their tales.

 OF DREAMS AND SHADOWS
OF HEART AND STONE
OF THORNS AND CURSES

THE KNIGHTS OF CAERLEON

AN ARTHURIAN LEGEND REVERSE HAREM FANTASY
Under J. Sundin

Four cursed knights. One warrior princess.
A faerie sword that binds their lives together.

THE FIFTH KNIGHT
THE THIRD CURSE
THE FIRST GWENEVERE

A HARTWOOD FALLS ROMANCE

CONTEMPORARY ROMANCES

Under Jae Dawson

MOONLIGHT AND BELLADONNA
HEARTBEATS AND ROSES SNOW-
FLAKES AND HOLLY

Thank You
Happy Reading!

Thank You Friends

**A dash of moon magic. A pinch of tree laughter.
Stories whispered on the wind.**

Hello Etsy wayfarers! Welcome to my bookish shop. When not slouched behind a computer, cursing the keyboard gods, you can find me frolicking through the woods with a camera around my neck or on the Comic Con circuit as MoonTree Books. Have fun poking around at my wares.

BOOKISH WARES FOR SALE

- Signed Paperbacks
- Limited Edition hardbacks
- Book Swag
- Book Boxes
- Custom Character Candles

Scan the QR code to visit my store.

Have questions? Message me on Etsy and we'll figure out your next fantasy adventure together.

JESIKAH SUNDIN is a multi-award winning Fae Romantasy, Dystopian Punk Lit, and Historical Fantasy writer, a mom of three nerdlets, a faeriecore and elfpunk geek, tree hugger, nature photographer, and a helpless romantic who married her insta-love high school sweetheart. In addition to her family, she shares her home in Seattle, Washington with a rambunctious husky-chi and a collection of Doc Martens boots. She is addicted to coffee, GIFs, memes, potatoes, cheese, kilts, mossy forests, eyeliner on men, and artsy indie alt rock.

www.jesikahsundin.com